Congrats on the giveaway.
I hope you enjoy my
book and the one J
picked for you.
All the best.
Anna-Kat ♡

PERFECT
SCARS

ANNA-KAT TAYLOR

COPYRIGHTS

Copyright reserved @ 2024 by Anna-Kat Taylor

All rights reserved.

No part of this book may be reproduced in any form or shape without written permission from the author except for the brief quotations in a book review.

The characters and events portrayed in this book are pure fiction. Any resemblance to places, events, or real people, living or dead, is entirely coincidental and not intended by the author.

ANNA-KAT TAYLOR

TRIGGER WARNING

This book contains adult content, including but not limited to violence, explicit language and sex scenes, crimes, killings, and rape.
It also brings up and touches on miscarriage and feelings after the loss of a child.
If you think you may be triggered by any of this content, please do not read this book.

ANNA-KAT TAYLOR

PERFECT SCARS

ANNA-KAT TAYLOR

*They say first loves hurt you the most.
I can only hope they're wrong.*

PART ONE

ANNA-KAT TAYLOR

ONE | NINA

Driving to the local hospital has brought up all kinds of memories for me from the time I lost my mother when I was 14 years old. That was over 10 years ago and today, I feel just as useless not knowing what's wrong with my baby sister and not being able to help her in any way.

Life can be a cruel bitch in some ways and take everything from you in the blink of an eye.

I never had a father to begin with or at least not one that I can remember and when my mom passed, I was left to take care of my sister, who is 5 years younger than me. She's the only living relative that I know of, and I protected her with everything I have, just as I will continue to do so until my last breath.

It may seem dramatic at 26 to say that but in my world, I made it a lot further than I was expected to.

Rihanna being my spirit animal, it's just normal that Rockstar 101 blasts in the speakers while I speed on the road surface like I'm immortal and I'm not driving just a huge metal cage.

Lost in my own head, I fail to notice the red light I'm speeding through and when I do, it's already too late and I briefly see the vehicle on my right before it crashes into my right wing.

It only takes a second for the airbag to pop and hit me in the face hard and for the car to start spinning uncontrollably. Luckily for me, this is what I do for a living, so I know how to quickly take back control and stop the car before it hits something else or worse, someone else.

"Well, shit!" The first instinct I get is to slam the gas and keep driving until I reach the hospital because the last thing that I want to do now is deal with some old fart wanting to get a shit ton of money from me to fix their Toyota. However, I don't run and decide to deal with the crap I've landed myself in but that is only until I turn my head to find the other damaged car, and what I find almost gives me a heart attack.

The car is definitely not a Toyota, but a fucking Camaro ZL1 which costs over 50 grand.

A fucking Camaro!

You've got to be kidding me.

It's exactly what I need right now.

"How the fuck did I get so lucky today?" I want to scream but whisper defeated instead.

I roll down my window to ask people not to call 911, but I don't get to make a sound before a huge figure appears at the side of my car and leans on my hood, blocking everything else.

"Can I help you?" I decide to get cocky and ask the stranger whose smoldering blue eyes seem to search my soul for a second before answering my question.

"Yeah, go get some more driving hours, you seem like you might need them to not kill anyone on the streets," he decides to offend me while smiling like the devil.

I have to admit, the position he sits in, towering over me with his huge build, makes me feel like a trapped mouse. With his perfect cheekbones and hard jawline, he just might be the devil.

A very beautiful devil.

"I'm perfectly capable of driving, thank you very much," I say through gritted teeth and turn my attention to the car, hoping that it will start.

After all, it wasn't such a big deal, and I'm pretty sure it could've been avoided if he's such a good driver.

For a long hot minute, he decides to not say anything and stares at me with the intensity of a detective. I would know that because I have been under the eyes of one more than a dozen times. But the intensity of his stare makes my skin heat up in ways that it hasn't before because none of the freaking detectives were this attractive.

"I feel sorry for your car. Real nice one, but it could do better on who drives it, sweetheart," he whispers after he's leaned so low on my window that I can basically smell his minty breath.

How the fuck am I turned on by this? I should be petrified. He's six foot tall for sure, has muscles like one of those crazy gym rats and he looks at me like he could swallow me whole.

Swallowing my retort, I decide to cut it short and get out of the way before someone else lost in their thought's bumps into me.

"Listen, buddy, my insurance will pay for the damage, here's my details, now I really loved the chat, but have got to run, so I hope I'll never see you again," I mumble quickly and before he can say anything else, I reverse like a pro, spin the car with way too much speed for a person who just hit their car, and continue on my way to the hospital.

When I quickly glance in my rear-view mirror, I cannot stop but admire the massive man with tattooed sleeves, standing tall with his 6'4', who's now smirking from the middle of the road, without any fear that he may be run over by another car. It makes me smile.

For the first time in a long time, I have a wide grin on my face, and for a brief moment, I wish I had stayed and at least got his name.

He definitely looks like a man who deserves a second glance.

I shake my head slowly and focus on the

driving, to make sure I don't do any more stupid shit for today. I smile at the thought of Mama not approving this type of guy. Mama would not approve of the type of lifestyle I'm living or the job I have, but when Carter Stark found me in a strip club looking for a job at 16, he decided that wasn't the path I was supposed to be on and gave me a slightly better option.

Or is it better?

I don't even know anymore.

What I do know is that I got out. I decided that stealing cars wasn't for me anymore and I took a step back. I enrolled in College, and I am close to getting my diploma in business.

Will it do me any good? I have no idea, but I felt like I needed something real and less fleeting in my life.

A constant, normal life like College, debts and a crappy apartment for me and my sister to live in.

I quickly realize that I have arrived at the hospital Jessica's in, and I park the car in the closest spot I can find. I turn off the engine faster than I ever have, and I bolt towards the entrance with a speed I didn't know myself capable of.

For a minute because of that guy, I almost forgot my priorities, but now that I am aware of my shitty life again, I have to find my sister.

At the reception, I stop in my tracks and ask quickly even if I'm out of breath, "Jessica Reeves, I'm looking for Jessica Reeves. I'm her sister, please tell me where I can find her."

"Sure, sweetheart. Hang on one minute for the system to open up," the nurse on duty replies with a smile, but how she called me irritates me more than it would have if that wasn't how the guy called me. "She's in room 47, but now she's doing some scans and should be back down soon," she adds after a brief pause.

I don't thank her, I just start walking towards the room she indicated, which is easy to find by following the signs and directions on the walls. However, when I arrive in front of the room, it is empty and Jessica is nowhere to be seen, so I enter inside and sit on the small armchair in the corner, hoping to get news soon.

"Miss Reeves?" I hear a man's voice call me and I realize that I am holding my face in my palms, so I raise my head and nod in answer while I rise on my feet.

"My Name is Dr. Richard Stone. I am sorry to be the bearer of bad news, but this cannot be sugar-coated. Miss Reeves, your sister fell today and although it was something insignificant, she had tremendous pain in her right knee when she was brought in, so we had to do a set of tests to rule out some possible diseases, but unfortunately, one of those possibilities became the truth. I am deeply sorry, but your sister has got Stage 2 bone cancer. I'm deeply sorry Miss Reeves." I'm sure I stopped listening midway on his explanation of what happened but coughed the part at the end of what was wrong with my sister.

I am aware that I remain quiet for a very long time but to wrap my head around what the doctor just said is a lot harder to do than one would think. "I need to see her," I whisper while a tear slides down my right cheek.

"Miss Reeves, we need to discuss treatment plans," he stops me before I bolt out of the room.

I swallow the hurt and the tears that want to stream down my cheeks and compose myself before asking, "Does she know?"

"No. Not yet." He replies with an understanding look on his face. I clench my jaw, blow out a deep breath, and whisper, "Good. I'll tell her. How much is it?"

It doesn't take long for the doctor to know what I'm asking, so he starts talking, "With insurance..." he doesn't get far because I have to stop him in his tracks by raising my hand.

"Doc, we both know that's not the case. So how much?" I say with bitterness in my voice.

It is the second time in my short life on this earth that I know the American health system will fail me.

The doctor knows it too because he gives me a pained smile before answering my question. "I'm sorry, Miss Reeves, but it could go up to 500 thousand dollars and as I'm sure you're aware, it won't guarantee anything. Cancer is a battle that many have lost."

That kind of money means I have to go back to

doing the one thing I hate in this world again.

Working for Carter Stark.

There goes my degree, my freedom and my normal life.

When I started working for Carter it was all very exciting for a teenager with a passion for cars, but it quickly turned dangerous and not as much of a fantasy anymore.

"I can provide you with health care advisors and any other support you may need Miss Reeves, so how do we proceed?" He asks me with the kind of understanding look that melts my bones away and as mad as I want to be at him for delivering such horrible news, I can't.

"You're asking me if I have that kind of money," I reply with a bitter tone.

"No, I'm asking if we should move your sister to a cancer clinic because after the test results come back, there's nothing more we can do." Before I get to answer that, my sister is brought into the room in a wheelchair, and I try my best to hold it together with an iron grip because one wrong word and I know I will crumble at her feet in a pool of tears and that's not what she needs right now.

She needs me to be strong and to be her rock, like always. She needs me to smile and tell her that everything will be all right.

"Nina, you're here," she whispers with a sad smile on her face. My sister was always the smartest one in the family and it's obvious she knows something's up.

"Of course, I'm here, Monkeyface, where else would I be?" I ask without actually waiting for an answer. She knows me better than anyone in the world and she sure as hell knows I'm not one not to care even if sometimes I wish I didn't because I'm not a good guy and the bad things I do, often haunt me.

"Stop calling me that! I'm 21 for Christ's sake." She retorts with an angry laugh. When she stops laughing, she sits there in silence for a moment, looking at her hands until she lifts her head to look me dead in the eyes, making sure I won't lie to her. "It's cancer, isn't it?"

Am I shocked that she figured it out? I'm not. She knows what mom went through and what tests she had done when we were told she had cancer. She remembers the pain our mom went through, and the heartbreaking screams and the soul wrenching hurls from chemo.

She remembers it all even if she was only 11 when mom died.

"I'm so sorry, Jess," I whisper and take her shaking hand into my own.

God, how I wish I could do anything to ease the heartbreak.

How I wish I could do anything to at least take her pain away. I can handle it, but she's my baby sister.

"Why would you be sorry? It's not like you gave it to me," she almost laughs in my face, but obviously, the situation doesn't let her.

She's always been a fun bubbly person and I love her for it. I love that despite being just the two of us, she was always a person I am proud to call my sister.

The one to raise my spirits when we couldn't make rent.

The one to make me laugh when a sad movie was getting to me.

"I'm sorry it had to be you to go through this. It should have been me." I plead with an invisible force, hoping someone will listen and change the roles.

She doesn't deserve this.

I can't go through losing her and I know that's selfish.

"Nina, don't go all big sister on me. Please! There's nothing you can do about it now, just accept it. I have. From the moment I walked inside this hospital, I knew it and I accepted it. You should too!" She whispers with a straight face, and it just shocks me how she hasn't shed a tear yet.

Humor has always been Jess's coping mechanism and I know, that when she's making too many jokes, she's deflecting.

"Accept what, Jess?" I ask carefully, not wanting to accept what she's asking of me because I know damn well what she's on about but refuse to acknowledge it.

"That I'm going to die," she deadpans on me,

and I remain still as a statue for a few long seconds.

I laugh it out, trying to cover how worried I am about everything because I am terrified of losing Jess. "You're not going to die, silly. You're stage 2 which means we have a shot at beating this. We have a real shot, Jess."

She sighs deeply before bringing out the issue we both thought of since the news broke. "I'm uninsured, Nina. How are we going to pay for any treatment?"

"It turns out, Carter Stark is the answer to our problems once more," I whisper more for myself and get lost down memory lane, at the time I met Carter and he changed the course of my life forever.

"But you don't like working for him, and plus, it's dangerous, Nina. You could end up in jail," she tries to remind me, but I already know all of these things. That's why I got out before it was too late last time.

I got out for her. I got out because I know I can't do this forever and always walk away unscathed. I am not bulletproof, or immortal and at some point, one of those will end up in my skull, that's why I got out. Because I didn't want to leave my sister alone in the world.

The thing is that Jessica doesn't know the entire story of my job. She has no idea that I kill people in the process of stealing cars, or she'll probably never want to see me again.

There are a million things that I had to protect her from because I never had anyone to protect me, or things would have turned out differently.

Worst thing? I don't mind doing it either. It's become my drug.

Stealing cars and killing has become as easy as breathing and I'm damn good at it.

TWO | BRODY

I should be mad.

I should be furious because the last time someone scratched my car, I went mental and slashed their tires, just so I didn't put a bullet in their head.

Today, however, I didn't do anything. I just stood there, wanting to chat with the girl with the sad green eyes for an eternity. I just stood there and gawked at her full lips, imagining how they'd feel if I'd kissed them.

I just stood there, like a lovesick pup, and took in her facial expressions and outlines.

I just fucking stood there, when I could've at least gotten her number for all the selfish reasons, but when her laugh warmed my insides and made me feel like I'd heard it before, I forgot what to do next.

My mother used to tell me that when you meet someone who makes you feel like you've known them forever, you have to hold onto that person for dear life because it means that in a different lifetime, we were important to each other.

Luckily before I get to dwell on my idiocy, I reach Carter's house and park on the drive. I turn off the engine and get out of the car, quickly sprinting towards the entrance. I know where to find the man of the hour, so I continue my walk toward the pool, he definitely has one. He always had one in any city he lived in because by his standards, that makes you rich, so It's exactly where I find Carter, who is enjoying a neat whiskey, and a blonde woman.

"Brody Mason, in the flesh. Did you miss me, old friend?"

I shake hands with my old friend and nod my head toward the blonde. "Good blowjob?" I ask, disgusted by the woman's appearance. Her red lips alone make me want to gag and remind me of why I never kiss a woman.

Is she a prostitute for fuck's sake? Carter used to be so much better at this.

"Killer. Listen, that's not why I had you travel all these miles to come to L.A. I have a huge job to pull together very quickly, and I need the best of the best. You in?" He simply asks and I smile sheepishly.

That is exactly what I need, a distraction and a few million dollars will most definitely not hurt my cause. "Fuck yeah, you know I'm in. I gotta keep it moving if I don't want to be found, so tell me, what have you got for me?"

I take a seat on the sun bed next to his and the woman hands me a glass half filled with whiskey. "Can you add some ice?"

"It's a few cars we need to steal. Not a big deal but we need a big budget so there's more shit before that. Anyway, I have to get some of the crew together, so I'm having a small party this Saturday. Unless you want to stick around? There's plenty more where she came from," he gestures towards the blonde, now blowing kisses at me, totally making me cringe.

I mean, I get it that this is what she does for a living, but at least stick to one man at a time.

I like a trio as much as the next person, but only if it involves two women who sleep with me because they want to, not because I'm going to pay them.

A quick fuck? Yeah, I'm always up to that too, but never with prostitutes. I'm sure I'll find something later tonight at this party of his but I sure as fuck won't stick it in a prostitute.

That's my golden rule.

Never fuck something that's been through more than a dozen dicks in one week and never kiss a woman if you don't know whose dick she sucked before yours.

I take a big gulp of the now-cooled drink in my hand. "Can't. Got some shit to sort out, a chick ran into me today and it's her number I need more than her money," I say with a wink and after an understanding nod from Carter, I walk back out the way I came in, towards my car, where the girl's insurance sits on the passenger seat.

I drive a manual, so I put it in first gear and drive off, back towards the apartment I rented as soon as I got in the city.

I'm very aware that Carter could've just invited me to the party over the phone, but he would never pass up the opportunity to show me what he's achieved with the Phantoms, his crew, the one he's been begging me to join for years.

I couldn't. My father would have never let me live outside of our family and laws. Just how he never let me be happily married to the woman I loved. If I hadn't distanced myself from them, I would never be able to do what I wanted to do for once.

He would always have a leash on me and when I killed the hand that held the leash, they decided to bring war over my head. So, I had to run and hide for the past 2 years, but now money's running low so Carter's call came as a blessing. I just hope they don't find me before I disappear again.

I suddenly realize that I'm back at the traffic lights where I've been hit this morning and that brings a dumb smile on my face. Why do I get the feeling that this woman will fuck me up... or better said, she could fuck me up because I'm sure as hell not letting another woman into my heart just so she can destroy it.

I can't go through that again and to be honest, I don't even know if I still have a heart for her to destroy.

I'm pretty damn sure I buried it with Eva.

I shake my head and take a deep breath before

pulling into the parking spot that came reserved with the apartment, grab the papers, and start walking toward the entrance.

Once I'm up, I grab my laptop first to check the camera feed. I've been in the city for a week now, but I couldn't meet with Carter before I had my safety checks and preparations, which basically means I found the cheapest neighborhood and rented the best apartment, which is not the luxury lifestyle I'm used to, but it should not raise questions.

Then I installed security cameras in the lobby and all around the building, without anyone asking any questions, which is great, I guess.

After I checked the camera feed and saw that no one suspicious was around while I was away, I went and picked up the girl's insurance and dialed the number on it. "Hi, I got hit by a lady today and she gave me her insurance but I'm pretty sure I might need her license for you to deal with it, so I was wondering if I could maybe get her number for now so I can get all the documents I need?"

"I'm sorry sir, I can't give you any information regarding our client due to confidentiality. I'm afraid I can't help you this time," she replies with a confident and friendly tone and proceeds to hang the phone which I'm sure is not standard procedure.

"Fuuck!" I swear under my breath and throw the insurance paper away. Well, this has led me nowhere, so what now? How am I supposed to find her because I'm sure as hell, that I won't let her sad eyes fool me when I know exactly what kind of woman she is.

I need to see her again.

I will see her again; I just have to find her ass first, so I grab my jacket and car keys once more and leave the apartment with a clear plan.

The insurance paper that she gave me has got the address of the insurance company, so if my charm won't work over the phone, I might as well try and make it work in person, so I step on the gas.

When I get to the small building, I park and exit the car in one swift move. I stroll toward the entrance and am very happy to find a young woman sitting at the desk. "Hi, beautiful. Name's Brody Mason, we spoke on the phone, about a woman who crashed into me and left me with serious damage. I brought the car if it'll help me get her number."

"Mr. Mason, I thought I'd been clear on the phone, that's just not the type of information I can give away. I'm sorry," she replies with a sad smile, and I have to breath quietly through my nose and contain my rage.

But I choose to take another route. "Listen, sweetheart, I'll tell you what. My car is a Camaro ZL1, and if you don't know much about cars, I'll just tell you that's an expensive one. A bit over 50 grand, so, I'll give you the honor of insuring it and getting the commission if you give me that fucking number."

She looks perplexed for a short time and I'm not sure if it's because of the car price or my language, but when she becomes all nervous, I understand it's the price.

I know a lot of the LA's cars are expensive, but a hefty commission in her pocket wouldn't be such a bad start to her day, plus, she does look a bit young, so that should make her a rookie. "Do we have a deal?"

She nods quickly and pulls out a pen and paper before inviting me over to one of the cubicles, so I throw her one of my most charming smiles.

After a few seconds of typing, she writes the name and number down and hands it over to me.

"Thank you," I say with a grin and grab the piece of paper. "I don't have my papers with me, but as soon as my car is fixed, I'll be back, ok? You have my word," I add with sincerity, and she nods in understanding. This was easier than I thought it would be.

God bless America.

This must be how telemarketers and surveyors get our numbers.

When I get back in the safety of my car, I pull out my phone and write a simple text.

THREE | NINA

It's 7 pm when I look at the clock on the apartment wall and I know I can't make any next steps into Jessica's treatment before I talk to Carter, but how the fuck do I do that after the way I left and promised him I'd never come back because I don't need his damn crew.

After I gingerly told him he can go fuck himself and that accepting to work for him was the biggest mistake of my life?

I left Jessica at the hospital to be monitored until I find a solution. I promised her I'd visit again tomorrow, and I hope that I get to keep my promise.

Funnily enough, in the next second my phone rings, and when I pick the phone up from my pocket, I smile when I see Carter's name in bold letters.

I owe you one big guy.

"What do you want Carter?" I ask with and exhausted breath.

This is not how I hoped my day would go. I was supposed to go to college as usual and just ignore everyone.

That's my routine.

"You, and you should damn well know it," he

replies from the other end and that makes me clench my jaw. If I have to sleep with him to get what I need, I will but I'll hate myself for it.

Carter is the last man on earth I'd ever touch.

Don't get me wrong. He's hot as hell and just as good looking but his attitude makes me want to throw up. He's always liked to be bossy and treat women like trash, so I could never stand that type of behavior.

"You have two seconds, Stark, so cut the crap," I say into my phone and sigh deeply.

"Come over this Saturday, I have some news and you'd want in on this," he adds before I end the call. He knows he needs to work hard to catch my attention but now he has no idea that I'm fucking desperate.

"Okay. I'll be there," I promise and end the call without waiting for anything from Carter. I know him well enough to foresee that now that business was over, he'd talk some more about us and what we could do together as a couple.

When he first offered me a job, I was 16 and he was 26, but that didn't stop him from trying to seduce me. For some reason, I've managed to keep him at a distance, and I am very glad and very proud of that achievement.

Carter is well known in the underground for the parties he throws in LA since we moved here with the Phantoms.

Yep, that's what we're called but the good thing is, we didn't name ourselves, the cops did. Every time some car disappears in the city, they blame us, regardless of whether we had anything to do with it or not.

Most of the time it was us, anyway.

Since I started working for Carter, we moved quite a lot around the country, making sure we were never in the same state for too long, so they never had any leads on us or who the leader was. I grew up in Denver and that's where I met Carter.

I think we lived in about 5 states since then and each time I had to ruin my sister's social life because of it.

Sometimes after a race, they'd catch a kid or two, but they all knew well enough what would happen if any of our names came out of their mouths, so they never said a word. Some even served a bit of prison time, just to keep our identities a secret, because they were paid damn well for it.

We made most of our money from stealing expensive cars, but we made good money from races too. Everyone knew that when we were out, they would see a good race, so the bets went wild and the rate for a race was always 2 thousand or more.

I grab the tea that I made myself and make myself comfortable on the sofa. I turn on the TV and let it fill in the quiet while I text Jess.

Me: Hey, how are you feeling?

Jess: Tired but can't sleep. What are you up to?

Me: Nothing much.

Jess: Did you speak with Carter?

Me: I did. He called me, so it wasn't as bad as I thought it would be. Turns out he has a job in Denver.

Jess: So, we're going home?

I can almost hear the excitement in her voice, so I sigh.

Me: I am. You have to get better first and if that's what you want, Jess, we'll move back to Denver.

Jess: I think I'd like that. ☺

I read Jess's text when I get the notification of a different one and open that first, curious as to who's texting me.

Unknown: You thought you were smart, but I'm smarter. You owe me and I'm going to collect.

What the actual fuck?
Who is this?

Unknown: You know I can see when you've read the message, right?

Okay, I'll bite.

Me: Who are you?

Unknown: A secret admirer.

Me: Hmm, not interested.

I quickly go to block him when another text comes in and weirdly, makes me smile.

Unknown: If you block me, I'll call the police.

Me: Is this supposed to be flirting? You're very bad at it. Who are you?

Unknown: A man whose heart you've broken.

Me: Aww, sounds rough.

Unknown: Huh, so you think you can pass me your insurance details, who by the way, suck, and forget about ruining my car?

Oh.

Me: Oh!

It's pretty blue eyes. I'll be damned. Now this is interesting. How did he get my number?

Unknown: As I said, you owe me, pretty girl. A date. The price is a date.

I know he can't see me through the screen, but I pinch up a brow.
This shouldn't thrill me, but it does.
After all, it's been forever since I've been asked out by a mysterious stranger.

Me: Coffee, tomorrow at 9 at Beans and Breakfast, on 5th Ave.

I reply and this dumb smile sticks on my face. I know I shouldn't do this, entertain this idea of dating when Carter has a job brewing and I'll be gone soon enough, but I have to see if the attraction is there, or it was just something temporary.

I want those fucking butterflies that everyone keeps talking about.

It's Tuesday, so that gives me 4 days to have some fun.

FOUR | BRODY

I reach the café she indicated a bit after half 8 and I take one of the quiet booths. A waitress comes over to greet me with menus and coffee, and I happily take a cup of black poison.

When she places the menu in front of me, I don't ask for a second one because I'm not a hundred percent sure that she'll show up.

In the end, she could think that I'm a creep and decide that it's not worth it, although if the way she was looking at me is any indication of how she felt, she'll show up.

And she does.

It's ten to 9 when she waltzes in, and I watch her say something to the barista before she spots me. When she does, she strolls over with a straight spine and takes a seat across from me.

"Hi," she says. "Okay, I'm here, so what can I help you with?" she adds and narrows her green eyes at me.

Damn, those are some beautiful eyes.

She isn't wearing a lot of makeup, just enough to accentuate them and to cover up the fact that she just woke up. "I just wanted to see you again. Can you blame me? You're so beautiful."

She snorts and I watch her eyelids fall closed

before she opens them back up and looks at me like I'm her breakfast.

I like that look.

The waitress returns with her coffee and a menu, which Nina slides beside her, uninterested.

"I don't even know your name."

"My bad. I'm Brody Mason, a pleasure to meet you," I say and put my hand forward. I have to admit, she surprises me when she takes it and shakes it slowly. Her small hand is warm against mine.

"Nina Reeves," she replies and takes her hand back. "I'm truly sorry about your car," she adds a beat later, and her face looks like it's never apologized before.

"Don't worry about it. It's just a piece of junk."

When her hand flies toward her heart and she mimics pain, I can't help but burst out laughing. I like her. "Your Camaro would be heartbroken if she heard you. You shouldn't talk like that about them. They have feelings, you know?"

"Why do I get a feeling you care more about your car than a person." Now it's my turn to narrow my eyes.

It doesn't matter anyway. I don't want a wife, I want her, in my bed, with me on top, and for however long I am in LA, I will try to make that happen.

See, as I mentioned before, I don't do prostitutes. I do beautiful women with curvy bodies and plump lips, like the woman in front of me.

"You're almost right. I care about someone more than I care about my car, but we're not friends, so I won't tell you my life story. Why am I here, Brody Mason?" she asks, and a bored look takes over her face.

I can't tell if she's truly bored, not interested in me or just playing hard to get.

"I thought we could get to know each other."

She laughs. "That's very cheesy, and you know it. We both know you want to fuck me senseless, but I'm not that kind of girl, so I'll save you the headache of trying to win me. I'll only be here for a week or two max, and then we'll part ways, so what's the point?"

"That's just one extra reason to let me show you a good time and then go our separate ways," I reply with a smirk, and by the annoyance I see in her green eyes, I know I won't get her so easily.

But I'm willing to work for it.

"Not happening, buddy, and you've wasted enough of my time," she says and raises onto her feet to leave.

"Can I at least text you once in a while?" I ask and she agrees with a cheeky wink before she leaves me staring at her long legs as she waltzes out of the café.

So, I take my phone out of my pocket and text her.

Me: Those legs are worth the headache.

She replies with a wink and a blushing emoji, and I smile like a teenage boy.

Game on, beautiful.

FIVE | NINA

When I step out of the café, I take a deep breath in and walk back to my car. I can't hide the fact that this man... he's a fucking catch and I can bet good money on his skills in bed. His eyes promise fun, while his smirk promises naughtiness and I want that. I want him to fuck me senseless, but something pulls me back and I can't tell what.

Maybe I just want him to work a bit before we close the deal. Or maybe he scares me because, in the end, he's just a stranger. The person whose car I wrecked and who didn't want money, just a date.

I'm truly curious where it could lead, but we don't have much time left, and something deep inside my soul, hates the fact that he only showed up now.

As I get at the wheel of my car, his text replays in my head. What did he mean that my legs were worth the headache? Like he'll do anything to have me?

I take my phone out and text Jess.

Me: Get your shit, I'm coming to get you.

With that, I drive off in the direction of the hospital, and just as I pass the café entrance, I see

Brody coming out. Our eyes lock for a second and after I salute him, I step on the gas and disappear.

Another text rings through and I ignore it, already guessing who it is from.

When I reach the hospital, I park near the entrance, and before I head inside to see if my sister is ready to go, I check the text I received while driving.

Unknown: You look hot behind the wheel. I bet you'd look even hotter behind my wheel.

I laugh at his text, but I'm not sure if he means his car's wheel or his dick.

Both prospects seem funny to me. I don't reply to him, but I do save his number and head for my sister's hospital room. When I walk in, I find her giggling like a schoolgirl at something she's reading on her phone. "Who's that?"

She's 21, but somehow, I still want to keep every guy away from her, like I'm an annoying older brother.

"Just Dylan," she replies with a blush.

"If your best friend makes you blush like that, then things are changing. Does he feel the same way?"

"I don't know, I never told him," she says, and her entire mood changes.

I sigh. "I'm sorry, I shouldn't have asked that with the current situation. Ready to go?"

"They're letting me out?"

"You're not in prison, Monkey, I'm taking you

out for a picnic in the garden," I say, and she throws a small pillow at me. A second later, her eyes narrow and she tilts her head sideways.

God, she looks so much like our mom that it almost hurts to look at her.

"You look extra nice and fresh. Spill it!"

"I met someone."

"When? How? You were here just yesterday," she frowns and looks excited, all at once.

"Yesterday morning. I ran a red light on my way here and he bumped into me, but obviously, it was my fault. He found my phone number and as payment he wanted a date with me, so we had coffee 10 minutes ago."

"That sounds stalkerish, but okay. Whatever fits your boxes," she says with a face that makes me laugh.

She grabs her bag, and we both head back to my car, the one whose right door is still banged pretty good and grab the stuff I grabbed this morning.

"So, are you interested in this guy?" she asks as soon as we make it to a patch of green.

The horrible thing is that I don't even have to think about this. "He's an arrogant ass, so yes, I am."

She laughs for a good minute. "You and your taste in men. You've met him a day ago, how do you know that?"

"Well, for one, he's hot and tattooed and he specifically said he wants to bone me. That equals an arrogant ass."

"In those exact words?"

"Not really. If I remember correctly, he said he wants to show me a good time, and my fucking pussy clenched at those words," I'm being honest and open with my sister.

We've always been like this because ever since she was younger, I had hoped that If I was honest, then she'd be the same as me.

"Well, maybe you should let him show you a good time, after all, you'll never see this guy again."

Funny how right and wise a 21-year-old can be. He is my one chance at some fun before we head off to Denver and God knows what will happen with us.

"Okay, enough about McDreamy, tell me what's with this special treatment," she speaks again a few minutes after we've laid the cover on the grass and we're both soaking in some sun.

McDreamy. I like that.

He is so fucking dreamy. Just picturing his broad shoulders flexing behind… Ugh, I shouldn't think of that right now.

"There's no special treatment. I'll probably go to Denver soon, you'll go to a cancer treatment clinic, and we don't know when I'll see you again, so the rest of this week is about you."

Jess doesn't say anything else, so we focus on enjoying the sandwiches and the warm sun.

SIX | NINA

Saturday came quicker than I would've liked, and it's already 6 pm.

I'm sure Carter is throwing one of his parties, so I head toward my closet to find something to wear. I'm not crazy about shoes or clothes for that matter, but I know they accentuate my body and help me seduce and destroy when needed. I go directly for a black tight dress, made entirely of wool and with strings at the sides. I take it out of the closet and hang it on my mirror to do my makeup first.

I choose to accentuate my green eyes with black smoky makeup and for my lips, I choose a dark brown matt lipstick, which makes them look even fuller. I smile at the image in the mirror, happy with the way it turned out, and get up to put the dress on.

I slide a pair of heels on, grab my leather jacket and when I look at the watch on my wrist and see that is almost half-eight, I make my way toward the door.

When I arrive at Carter's place, I cannot find any parking spot on the road, so I decide to try inside, but soon realize that a douche bag is parked in the way, blocking the access. Funnily, it's a Camaro, so I decide I hate this car and push it a bit out of the way to be able to enter.

When I'm successful with my plan, I park on the lawn, next to a Honda Civic Type R, the first car I got when I first started working for Carter.

I smile in nostalgia and after I lock my baby, I start walking toward the entrance. There are people everywhere in the living room, some dancing, some kissing, and some... I don't want to know, although I wish I was doing what they were doing right now, so I continue on my path until I reach the pool at the back.

I spot Carter chatting to a girl and I want to head in his direction, but I'm stopped in my tracks by a guy behind me. "Bro, you should see your car, someone bumped you from behind and your number plates are on the ground," he speaks with a shocked although amused tone, and it doesn't take long before I know who the guy behind me is speaking to.

It isn't another Camaro.

It is *the* Camaro.

Brody Mason's Camaro and now staring me dead in the eyes is the same gorgeous man who owns it. The man who's been texting me all week trying to seduce me and who's now sprawled in an armchair, with one girl at each side, but the look he gives me could ice over hell if it existed.

I truly hope it doesn't exist though, because then I would know where I'm headed after this, and being apart from mom and my sister for an eternity is just not very appealing to me.

I smile arrogantly because I can't let him see how much he affects me and cross my arms over my chest before he talks. "It was you? Again?" he asks with a serious tone and gets up in one swift movement.

He strides over, radiating menace and confidence, and as soon as I'm facing him, only a few inches between us, I know I should turn around and forget about the job Carter has because this man is trouble, and I am in a shit ton of trouble as it is. But no. I stand here, rooted on the spot, with the same bitchy attitude, trying to hold myself together so he doesn't see deep into my soul.

He's way taller than me and having to raise my head to meet his eyes doesn't help my case but I still manage to bite back, "You parked in my way?"

He chuckles and oh My, did I just get electricity running down my spine?

He shouldn't be here. We weren't supposed to meet again, but what are the chances that we both know Carter?

I'm in more trouble than my mind even realizes right now because when he shows his dimples in one of his dashing smiles, I part my lips and draw in a shaky breath and clench my thighs.

In the next second, he does the most intriguing and unexpected thing a man I just

PERFECT SCARS

bumped into his car, a second time, could do.

He smashes his lips into mine with such force that it knocks the breath out of me, but he doesn't give me time to process what's happening and soon I find myself melting in his arms and giving in on whatever he's doing to me. He makes me forget everything around me and I raise my hands to touch his hair. Since I saw him for the first time, I wanted to find out how his hair felt between my fingers.

He then grabs my hips with his big palms and draws me closer to him until I feel the erection that's come alive in his pants, and I moan. I moan into his mouth, and I swear his dick twitches at the sound I make and his grip on my hips tightens.

God, he was right. He can definitely show me a good time with what he possesses in his pants.

As much as I enjoy his wandering tongue in my mouth, we are quickly interrupted by Carter who makes one of his stupid jokes. "You're barely back in town and you're already stealing my girl?"

Brody quickly believes Carter because he lets go of me in one swift move and pulls back a step.

Annoyed and frustrated by the interruption, I take control by catching his hand and pulling him back. Then I take a step closer and wrap both hands around his neck to pull him back in for a passionate kiss, that I hope makes him understand I'm no one's girl.

"Don't listen to him, Carter has been on my case for almost 10 years now, and nothing's ever happened," I whisper on his lips and his eyes sparkle in a way that makes my body heat.

Knowing that I won, I turn around and head for the bathroom, leaving the two men to deal with it but I don't make it into the bathroom before he catches up with me and grabs me by my waist before I get to open the door and turns me around. "You aren't going to leave me like this, are you?" he asks with an arrogant smirk on his face while he pushes my back onto the wall.

I swallow the lump in my throat and try hardly to ignore the clench of my pussy. I should be annoyed by the way he implies that I owe him something or the demanding tone of his voice, but I push all those thoughts at the back of my head and wrap my arms around his neck.

It's crazy the type of chemistry and attraction that passes between us and how a mere minute ago I was wishing I did exactly this. I want to get laid and this guy looks like every girl's next mistake.

"Is that a dare, Brody Mason? You want to see how long I can resist your bad boy charms?" I whisper seductively and I throw my hips forward, but I didn't expect to be on the sink in the next second, with my legs wrapped around his hips.

Damn, does it feel good... I can't even remember the last time I had sex or felt this turned on by the erection of a man. The fact that they can get turned on by any bimbo always grossed me out, but Brody has been sending me texts all week, writing in detail all the things he would do to worship my body, so I guess the pressure has been building on and now I'm just dreaming that he wasn't all talk.

"I think it's been long enough," he says with a chuckle and kisses the side of my jaw setting my nerves on fire.

"I think so too," I whisper with a smirk of my own while I start unbuckling his belt. When it's easier to get access to what I want, I thrust my right hand into his pants and grab his massive cock, receiving a masculine gasp from Brody, and a curse in a foreign language that wasn't loud enough for me to understand.

"I thought I'd never see you again," he says on my lips, making me release a feral snarl.

"Shut up and fuck me," I demand with a grin and go back to kissing him. It doesn't take long for Brody to free his dick from his pants, the length of it pressing against my stomach. Oh, how I wish I was naked to be able to feel it on my skin, but just the thought of that makes my toes curl in excitement.

Brody then raises my dress over my hips and penetrates me in one swift move that makes my head go blank at the feel and length of it.

I'm not sure if it's really been that long or he's just so fucking good but this is fucking delicious.

I grab onto his neck to steady myself on the sink and start rotating my hips to meet his thrusts while our moans fill the bathroom.

Well, I have to say, I've never been fucked in a bathroom before, so that's a plus.

"Tell me what you want, baby," he whispers in my ear and slows down the pace, making me completely lose my mind.

My skin is on fire, and I can barely put together words to formulate what he asks of me. I want so many things. I want him to kiss me again. I want him to touch me, but I can't say anything.

I can definitely say that he fucked my brains out.

"You're so fucking beautiful," he adds, and his hand presses between us until it reaches my clit and begins circling it. Those words alone could make me come undone, but I want to savor the moment and refuse to let my body control this.

"Right there, don't stop," I manage to breathe, and he continues as asked while also moving his hips in rhythm. I clench around him and keep my legs tight around his torso, helping him reach so high that my back arches.

"Say my name," he says while reaching that point with his cock that very few men do and that makes me see stars, so I close my eyes. "Eyes on me, baby," he adds in a growl, and I quickly snap my eyes to his.

"Don't stop, Brody," I beg, answering his command and after a few deep thrusts, my climax begins to cloud my vision and I quickly melt into his grip, unable to hold onto his shoulders anymore.

"Can you take my cum, baby?" He asks in a low groan and, my body shivers in pleasure at the way he asked the question so when I nod frantically, he quickly follows me with his release, deep inside of me, with a growl that makes my body shake with pleasure and excitement. "God, you're amazing, woman, just like I thought you'll be," he adds in a whisper as he rests his sweaty forehead on top of mine.

I almost don't want to let go, but after we've both caught our breath, he releases me and shields his semi-hard cock back in his pants, so I decide to do the same, jump off the sink and pull down my dress.

"I have to admit, that was the best fuck I had in a long time," he says after pulling his zipper up.

"Thanks?" I reply with a frown, unable to read him. I turn around and try to tame my hair a little before going back out, although everyone can easily guess what we've done.

He smiles and completely punches me in the gut with the next question, "I don't even know your name, do you do this often?"

I scoff and raise a brow. Should've figured he'd be another dick. "It's Nina Reeves and if you expect me to ask for money, it's not my type," I spit the words at him and start walking toward the door, but he grabs my hand before I make it too far.

"No, I'm sorry. I shouldn't have said that. You just... surprised me, that's all. I wasn't expecting you to be so... good in bed," he says apologetically, and I decide he deserves a chance.

I scoff again. "This was hardly a bed."

"There's one across the hall," he replies with a grin on his smug face.

"Sorry to interrupt, cowboy, but I need my girl for a minute," Carter speaks to Brody and I roll my eyes.

"I am not your damn girl, Carter!" I shrug it off and start following him toward his office, leaving Brody behind me and hoping that he doesn't assume something's going to happen just because I was so quick to do it with him.

"Nina, you know I like you. I always have and always will. You are an important part of our team and you've earned your place among us. I would've expected you to come to me first if you needed help," he says with a concerned look on his face.

It makes me pinch my brows together in confusion. "I'm not sure I follow, Carter."

Before going on, he sighs deeply and looks me deep in the eyes, "I've heard about your sister. I'm sorry to hear about what she's going through, but I can help. Come back to work for me and I'll make sure she gets all the treatments she needs."

Shit! He just left me without my advantage.

"Just like that? You have a job, don't you? I

know you don't do that out of the goodness of your heart. You barely give a shit about us, even less about our loved ones."

"Why do you say that? I always had a thing for you. You're that girl I could never have."

"And you never will. I don't sleep with crew members. So?"

He nods and relaxes into his chair.

"I do have a job and I need you as much as you need the money," he replies, and I swallow the lump in my throat.

This is not how I wanted things to go and I'm pretty sure I'm utterly fucked.

"Okay, let's hear what you have to say."

"Yes, but first I need you to promise me something. I'll make sure that Jessica gets the best treatment in the country and that's not here. That's in Rochester, Minnesota. I know someone there and they'll take good care of Jess."

As soon as I realize what he's saying I jump out of the chair and point an accusatory finger at him. "You want to send my sister all the way across the country? No fucking way I'm doing that when she needs me. You are out of your mind if you believe that."

"Yes, it's exactly what we're going to do. If you want what's best for her, you'll listen to me carefully, Nina. I don't want any complications with his job and Jessica, I'm sorry but she's a complication for me. You said it yourself, I don't give a fuck about your loved ones, but I need you, so if you want in on this job, we'll send Jessica to the best hospital in the country, where she'll be in safe hands, and you'll detach from all of it. I need you as focused and clear-minded as possible on this."

I know what he's asking but I refuse to acknowledge it or accept it. I cannot send my sister away and forget about her when she needs me the most.

No fucking way!

"What are you asking of me, Carter, is absolutely heartless," I whisper and wait for the confirmation of him taking full advantage of the situation.

"I'm asking you to trust me and forget that you have a sister for the next few months," he replies with a serious face and waits for my reaction.

I don't have one.

I don't trust Carter. Not with my sister's life but I also know I have no other options.

I have no one to ask for help. I have no one to have my back and even though I'm not Carter's biggest fan, he's always had my back. They all have.

"Okay. I'll do it." I say and as soon as the promise is out my mouth, I feel just like I've signed my life away to the devil.

Maybe that's exactly what I've done.

***

When a knock on the door breaks the silence, I just close my eyes and take a deep breath.

"Come in," is Carter the one to speak and I'm glad this room is far from the party in the other house so I can enjoy the quiet in my head.

I get up from my chair as soon as the gang has entered the room and greet each one of them. I am truly happy to see them, but I always hoped it'd be over a coffee, not a job.

But when Brody is the last one to enter, I feel my world collapsing around me.

I knew he'd be the biggest mistake of my life, but I'd. just hoped it wouldn't happen so soon.

No, no, no. He can't be part of the team. We can't work together after what we'd just done in the bathroom. "What's he doing here?" I ask pointing at the stranger who was deep inside of me a few minutes ago and who's name I was moaning.

"He is an old friend of mine, and now he is a part of the crew. We need everyone for the job I have," I get the answer that I hoped would be different.

Fuck!

There goes my rule about not sleeping with crew members because I had just fucked one and enjoyed it more than I'd like to admit.

I enjoyed it so much that I'd hoped it would happen again, which now seems unlikely.

It can never happen again!

It's too risky.

Like the bastard he is, Brody winks at me, so I groan and ignore his ass for the time being. I'll figure this out later.

I move my attention toward my old crew, people I've missed and love as family. Levi is the first to hug me tightly, like a brother and I always loved the way his arms felt around me. They make me feel protected and safe. "Welcome back, sweetheart," he says with a grin and kisses my forehead. Somehow, that makes me smile dumbly and I almost blush.

"Thanks, Levi. I missed you too," I wink at him and let go of his arms. Levi is the douche that always makes jokes to lighten a mood but will also always be the one to get you out of shit. I can always trust him to have my back.

As I move to greet Jax and Jason, the twins, I see Carter sitting on his desk, a power move I always hated at him. "It's so good to see you boys," I say in a motherly voice, something I know always pisses them off because they're only a couple of years younger and way smarter than me. They're pretty much the nerds of the team, the best in computing.

"You think if I make you moan my name, you'll stop calling me a boy?" says Jason when I hug him, and I'm happy no one else hears.

"In your dreams," I laugh and proceed to hug Simon, the only one left in the room. "Hi big guy," I add with a big smile on my face, one that he returns.

Yes, I'm the only girl in the group but that's never made me feel left out in any way. If it's done anything, it actually made me feel more protected. Almost like a princess when I couldn't be further away from being a princess in distress.

After I'm done saying hi to my guys, I walk toward the armchair and make myself comfortable.

Brody follows suit and I raise a questioning eyebrow when he sits on the side of my armchair, totally towering over me and making me feel small.

"Okay, now that you've kissed and made out, we can get to business. So, here's the thing. I've caught wind of 3 stunning Bugatti's, La Voiture Noire, which are going to pass through Aspen, Colorado in order to get to Canada to a multimillionaire and his two sons and of course, I couldn't pass onto such an opportunity. We're going to steal those beauties from under their nose," he explains, and I find myself doubting every word he says.

Carter is usually very good at finding cars for us to steal if we're not actually being hired for that. But 3 Bugatti's? That's over the top.

That's like the gold medal for the Olympics and I always dreamed of being in the Olympics, but it's also very dangerous and unpredictable.

"That's bullshit, Carter. La Voiture Noire is a unique model. Whoever told you there were 3 of them, played you," I hear Simon and I quickly turn my attention to him. It doesn't sound like Carter to miss things like this.

That's why we always got away with our jobs, because he's a genius at making plans, even if sometimes I hate to admit it.

I like to pretend he's just another stupid jock, but he's always been the brain of our operations because he's brilliant. He started stealing cars when he was 12 and never stopped since. He says that money always run low at some point and he could stop doing this anyway because it's like a drug for him.

"It was a one-of-a-kind car, but Devi Brown wanted so much to gift the same car to his twin sons, so he ordered two more cars, paying a shit ton of money for them. These 3 cars together are worth over 300 million in Mexico and if we can grab them, we're set for life. We could be done with small steals. This could mean we can finally retire the Phantoms once and for all. For real this time, I promise."

I weigh on Carter's words for a long time and by the way the entire room is silent, it seems like everyone is doing the exact same thing.

I lift my head to gaze at Brody and I see his jaw ticking, which could mean a thousand things right now. Who is he, though? He seems close to Carter, but I've never seen him before, or heard his name, so where did he come from?

"And you want to do this hit with 7 people?

That's madness, and you know it. Count me out," I decide to speak out and I see a few of them agree with me.

I need money more than I need air, but this won't get us the money, it'll get us time in prison. It'll clearly be our last job because we'll get caught.

"Nina, please, hear me out. We can't do this without you. You really want to say no to a few million dollars in your situation?"

I hear the hint of a threat in his voice, and I don't like it one bit. I jump onto my feet and launch at him, only stopping when I'm close enough to face him. This is one of the moments when I hate that we don't have the same height. These fucking guys are monsters, and they're all above 6 feet, so my 5'7 has nothing on them. "Wait a damn minute! A few million? The cars are worth over 300 and I get a few million? Carter, have you completely lost your damn mind, or do you really think I'm that desperate?" I shout through clenched teeth, and I try really hard not to punch him.

Because if I punch him, I might not stop. I've been holding in a lot of anger toward this guy for ten years now and a punch or two might not do it.

"If I remember correctly, you left us. You decided you're too good for us and left us, so yes, a few million is all I can offer for your services, Nina." Carter decides to attack me publicly and I can't say it shocks me.

He's always been the one who hated me the most for leaving the crew and I can't blame him for it. We were good and unstoppable but that's exactly why I decided to stop because I felt like my luck would run out on me.

"Then I'm out. I don't want any part of it if I won't be treated fairly," I say quietly and I start heading toward the door when Brody's voice stops me.

"What can you do for more than a couple of million, sweetheart?" he asks with an arrogant voice and when I turn to face him, I see his wicked grin.

I can't say it shocks me entirely, I know men like Brody Mason, and I should have stayed away from men like Brody Mason.

"To make you come in less than 5 minutes is not my only talent, sweetheart," I reply with a sweet smile and a wink at the end although deep inside I want to rip his head off.

This is exactly why I don't sleep with crew members because then they start to belittle you just because of those 5 seconds of pleasure. They start undermining you and think less of you because you're a woman, when I can bet a few million that this guy can't even race properly.

SEVEN | BRODY

She stands tall in front of me, and I swear to God I can feel my cock twitch in my pants. Her attitude makes me hard as fuck and I can already see how this will become a problem.

I know it was a dick move to say that after I've just had my cock deep in her tight pussy, but I couldn't help it. I love it when she becomes all flustered and angry.

A shiver runs through me when I remember how good she feels wrapped around me.

Who the fuck would have ever thought that the girl that I hit on the road and became my obsession will also be the girl that's in Carter's team?

"I'm not doing this with you," she says with clenched teeth.

Oh, but she is. Because this job means everything to me and it's obvious that me and Carter have the biggest cuts because we're putting together the whole shit show and they execute the orders.

"Listen, *baby girl*, you're nice and all that but that doesn't mean you'll get as much as we do, meaning that you have exactly 5 seconds to accept it or get out," I reply with a nonchalant stance and proceed to show her the door. I have to say that I'm excited to see how she reacts this time.

Her attitude and personality keep me entertained and I have to admit, if she does leave, I might miss her feisty attitude.

I don't know how important she is for the Phantoms, but I'm shocked when Carter stops her from leaving. "How much do you want?"

I know I'm usually good at keeping a straight face, but the way she's searching every inch of skin until her gaze reaches my eyes, I'm starting to doubt my skills.

"60 million," she answers with a stone-cold face and that makes me chuckle.

I have to admit, she has balls. She has more balls than these fuckers together, who haven't said a word since this conversation started.

"You know damn well that's not possible. We don't even know the price we'll be offered for them. I said an approximate price and you know that." Nina is now negotiating only with Carter, and I have to admit, it makes my blood boil in my veins.

I started this conversation. I should be the one to put an end to it, damn it!

"Okay. I'll tell you what I want if we don't know how much you'll sell them for. I want us all to get equal amounts because we're all an important piece of this job and you know it."

Suddenly I get an idea through my head and

that spreads a grin on my face. I walk slowly toward the woman who is waiting expectedly. "I'll give you 10 million from my cut if you kiss my hand," I say when I'm inches away from her.

I watch her like a hawk when her cat eyes start descending to where I hold both my hands, in front of my crotch, my body heats up in anticipation.

"I'm flattered that you offer me 10 million to mimic a blowjob, Brody Mason," she replies with a smirk on her full lips. However, she proceeds to bend until her lips are less than an inch away from my hand and although I feel inclined to remove my hands, I'm taken by surprise by what she does next.

Nina raises so quickly that I almost miss the fact that she points a gun at my head. "Good thing I don't need anyone's charity," she adds and hands me the gun. I examine it closely with a frown, only to realize that it's my own damn pistol. When I draw my right hand behind me to check, it's a confirmation that somehow, she picked that up without me feeling anything.

"Impressive," I mutter to myself and smile like a dork when if I want to win this battle, I should not do.

"Take this too, you might need it later when the cops pull you over," she continues her demonstration and hands me my wallet next.

I can't say she doesn't impress me and damn, she's been doing it since the moment I laid eyes on her this morning. "Why would the cops pull me over?" I ask with a raised brow, voice etched in curiosity.

I also do realize that we're having a conversation like no one is in the room, while I'm fully erect and bulging my pants.

She doesn't answer, instead, she grabs the gun back from me, takes two steps toward the window, and shoots two fires making the glass shatter with a horrible noise. "Because driving without taillights is illegal in LA."

"You are one hell of a woman, I'll give you that," I whisper.

"You asked what I can do for so much money, so I just showed you all the things I can notice, and you don't. Now I'm going back there to dance. You know where to find me when you make up your mind," Nina says to no one in particular and exits the office. I can't help but notice how Levi quickly follows her, wrapping an arm around her waist and something twists inside of me when she doesn't react and looks all comfortable with him.

I'll break that arm off one day, that's a promise.

"Okay, I admit she's a badass, but still, we can't really pay everyone equally," I say as soon as everyone has cleared the room.

Carter sighs and runs a hand through his hair.

"Listen, Mason, I know you and you know me, but you don't know Nina. There's no way we can do this without her and her Romanian roots, so yeah, we'll pay everyone equally."

Understanding that I might've messed up big time, I decide to drop it. "One more thing, the red-haired guy, how important is he to the team?"

Carter chuckles. "Who? Levi? Listen, man, stay away from him. He won't do anything if Nina doesn't allow it, but it's better you won't either. I need your heads in the game, buddy, so whatever you've got going on, it has to stop."

I nod and leave the room, needing to find Nina. The problem in my pants is persisting and I won't leave here with a boner, no matter what Carter says.

Back in the main house, I find Nina in the middle of the dancefloor, with Levi behind her, hands on her hips and I get the urge to growl. I quickly stride toward them and pull her away from his grip which wins me an angry look from the brunette but that doesn't stop me.

"Mmm, you smell so good," I whisper in her hair and wrap my arms around her tiny body. She's definitely not fragile, but damn does she feel fragile.

All I want to do is fuck her and protect her from myself, all at once and I'm not sure it's such a good combination.

"It's called perfume," she replies and turns her back on me, but that only brings her ass on top of my crotch and makes me go crazy.

"I can tell it's an expensive one."

"What do you want, Brody?" she asks but doesn't turn around or push me away, she continues to move her body, without realizing the pain she's causing me. So I push my hips forward to show her the situation she created between my legs and that's when she turns around furiously and pushes me in the chest.

"Seriously? Now you pretend you don't want me anymore?" I laugh nervously and step forward to touch her, but she evades my arms with a swift move.

"Go fuck yourself, asshole," she shouts and raises her hand to slap me but fails because I catch it with my own.

I bring her hand to my lips and kiss it softly. "I think I'd prefer it if it were you fucking me."

She just breaks free, spins around, and leaves me in the middle of the dancefloor, making me laugh by myself.

This woman... will be the death of me, but I kinda enjoy it.

EIGHT | NINA

I drive in silence, pestering in my own intrusive thoughts until I get to my apartment building. After I finish parking the car, I realize that I parked next to the landlord's car, and I wonder why he could be here at this hour.

I get out of the car, lock it, and run toward my apartment, hoping that I can sleep without thinking of broody Brody.

"Mister Han? What are you doing here at this hour?" I ask my landlord, who's in front of my apartment and the door is wide open.

"Miss Reeves, I have some bad news. I have sold the apartment and it has to be ready in 2 days," he spits in my face or at least I think he does because I am too shocked to register anything.

"What? What are you talking about?" I shout, very close to punching the guy.

Today is not a good day to piss me off.

"I'm sorry, Miss Reeves. I arranged for someone to pack the place up for you to pick up tomorrow, but you can't stay here tonight. I'm truly sorry."

The worst part of what he's saying is that he's not sorry, he's just a lying asshole. The bastard is enjoying this, and I might find it hard to not put a bullet in his head later.

"That's fucking insane, you know that right? I'll sue the hell out of you for this," I step closer and threaten him.

"No, you won't, because we both know how you can afford that car back there," he says and I'm not sure if he thinks I'm either a prostitute or a drug dealer.

What I'm doing is worse.

Fuck this!

I can't deal with this shit right now, so I leave. I leave because if I don't, I might do something I'll regret, and I can't go to jail right now. My sister needs me.

I get back to my car, climb onto the driver's seat, and grab the wheel with both hands like my life depends on it. I blow out a long breath and reverse into the parking lot, hoping to find a darker and quieter spot to sleep in because it is obvious that I won't have a bed to sleep in.

Once I find a spot that seems good enough for tonight, I park again, block my doors, and roll my chair all the way back. I'm not sleeping in the backseat because that's worse than the front seat.

I will find something tomorrow, tonight I just need to get the blue-eyed man out of my system. As soon as I think of his eyes, someone startles me with a knock on my window, so when I lift my head to check who's disturbing me, I find the exact man I was thinking about on the other side. "What are you doing here, Brody? You following me now?" I ask him as soon as I roll down my window and his scent hits me, making it really hard to concentrate.

"Are you sleeping in your car?" He asks with a concerned look on his face. He's making it really hard to hate him at this moment. What's with the 2 personalities for fuck's sake?

I open the door and climb out of the car trying to put some space between us.

"Was surely planning to until you interrupted me," I reply with anger, hoping that he'd drop it and leave me be soon. "What are you doing here, Mason?"

"You're not answering my question, Reeves and I'm not going to repeat myself, baby."

Oh, the nerve!

This fucker knows what kind of things he does to me with how he's speaking. "Why do you care?" I ask while massaging my temple, feeling a migraine sneaking in.

"I don't," he replies but even from a distance, I can finally see it in his eyes.

Fear.

Confusion.

He is terrified of whatever is happening between us.

Maybe I should be too.

"He kicked me out," I say in defeat.

I really can't fight him anymore. At least not today.

"Who? Your boyfriend?" He spits the words like they're poison, and I have to exhale deeply before answering him.

Is he actually pretending to be jealous?

"Come on, Brody. Cut the jealous boyfriend crap, it's not it for me. You know I don't have one. The landlord. He sold the place without giving me any notice in advance," I find myself explaining even though I don't owe him an explanation. Should've just let him believe it was my boyfriend. Could've been the solution to all the future problems he might create.

"You could've called Carter, you two seem close enough."

I shake my head and bite the inside of my cheek. This man is impossible, how will I ever work with him?

"I could but I won't. Plus, we're not close. Carter doesn't care about anyone else other than himself. He already has leverage on me, so I won't give him some more," I reply and wrap my arms around my body.

"Come here," he says suddenly and comes rushing forward. He then wraps his arms around me before I have a chance to say anything. "You're such a pain in my ass, you know that?"

I am a pain in his ass? Jesus...

"The feeling is mutual," I whisper in a muffled voice, my nose buried in his shirt. My God this feels good. Smells great too.

If this is what hell feels like, then I can die right now because I fucking feel the safest I ever had felt in my life.

"Come stay with me tonight," he takes me by surprise when he says that like he doesn't even need an answer.

How is it possible that I hate and love that about him at the same time?

"I can't. It's not who I am, Brody. I don't sleep around or use sex for my gain," I try to explain once I get free from his embrace and take a step back. I need to put some distance between us because he is intoxicating.

"I like the way you think, but that's not what I said. I said you're staying at my place tonight, nothing more. I have a free room with a very comfortable bed in it. I promise I won't do to you anything you don't want me to."

I ponder his words for a long time before making a decision. This definitely sounds like the start of a very bad mistake, but on the other side, what can I do? He will be my crew member so I might as well learn to work with him.

"Okay," I agree.

"Okay. Let's go then. Leave your car, we'll pick it up tomorrow," he orders, and I can't stop myself from snapping back at him.

"You afraid I'll run and hide from you?"

"What you chose to do is your problem, Reeves, I only want to help and it's your decision if you trust me or not," he shrugs it off and I'm left wondering if he's telling the truth or not.

"I'm not a kid, Mason. Of course, I don't trust you!"

"Smart girl," he chuckles. "Let's go, it got a bit chilly."

Will this be another huge mistake in 24 hours? Probably.

"I can't leave my car, I have somewhere to be tomorrow morning. Do you mind if I follow you?" I ask and he agrees.

I jump at the wheel of my car just as Brody takes off and I can stay closely behind him. Although it's very late, LA's streets are still very busy, so I try to keep as close as possible.

When we stop at the traffic lights, I decide to pull up on his left, and with a cheeky smile plastered on my face, I raise an eyebrow in challenge. Brody's eyes narrow for a second, but then a naughty smile takes over his clean-shaven face and we get ready to race.

I turn my attention to the lights and grip the leather steering wheel with determination, a surge of adrenaline coursing through me as I shift into first gear and take off as soon as the light turns yellow. My baby's engine roar echoes my determination as I navigate the not-too-crowded streets.

We don't have a set track as we'd have on a street race, so I take a hard left, forcing Brody to follow me. When he starts overtaking me, my eyes meet his, and my heart skips a beat, because as he keeps steady in line with me, something passes between us.

Although he's trying to take the lead, I refuse

PERFECT SCARS

to be beaten by a newbie, so I force it and move in front of him. With a speed reaching 260km per hour, I release a command to my car and call him. "Hey, we don't have a finish line, so let's call it a tie and follow me, I want to show you something."

He laughs but agrees with me, so I take him up to my favorite spot.

We make it up the hill in less than 20 minutes and we both park our cars side by side facing the city down below. I exit mine and pop up on the hood, as I'm used to doing since I learned how to drive.

Brody follows me and he sits right next to me, but he just leans on the car, arms crossed over his chest.

"Quite the race, huh? I didn't expect you to take a left like that," he breaks the silence, but I continue to take in the view.

"Thanks, you're not so bad yourself. I'm sure you could do some damage on a track. It was fun though," I reply with a hint of a smile.

I'm lying, it was more than fun. It was thrilling.

And I fucking missed it.

"This view is something else, isn't it? Makes a huge city look so small," he says, and it takes me a second to realize that he's turned his attention on me our eyes now locked with a lingering intensity.

"It's my favorite place on earth. I'm going to

miss it," I sigh and force a smile on my face.

"You're never coming back?"

I shrug. "I don't know... My sister wants to move back home."

"What do you want?"

I think long about his question and unfortunately, I don't have an answer because what I want is not important right now.

Suddenly it feels like he's closer than he's been a minute ago and my breath hitches when he grabs my legs, pulls me further down on the hood of my car, and stands just between my thighs.

Since when is this a turn-on?

He then cups my face and kisses me slowly, like he wants to memorize the feel of my lips, and I let him.

NINE | NINA

When we get to Brody's apartment, I am surprised to find a clean and organized place but regardless of how nice this place is, I shouldn't have accepted to come down here.

My gut feeling is telling me to turn around and run for the heels because Brody is definitely not the kind of guy to not try anything, even if he said he won't do anything I don't want him to, but that's the problem.

What if I want him to? Can I still blame him after?

"So quiet all of a sudden, you forgot your tongue in your car or are you afraid of me?" he asks when we reach the living room and I sit down on the sofa.

I almost want to sink into it and make myself small. "I'm exhausted, that's all. Your place is nice though," I say in complete honesty.

I don't think I can tell him about Jessica, but that's still a piece of the truth. It's been a long fucking day and I have a feeling that tomorrow will be even longer.

I have a feeling that every day from now on will be fucking long and exhausting.

"Make yourself at home, beautiful," he replies

and proceeds to pour us some whiskey. I close my eyes for a moment and play in my head all the ways in which I get to tell Jessica how she's got to do this by herself if I want to be able to pay for everything.

Brody enters a room behind one of the tree doors lined up on the right side of the apartments and returns holding a huge T-shirt in his hand. "I assume you want out of that dress?"

"I assume you want to take it off me?" I ask with a raised brow and a smirk while he hands me the piece of clothing.

He growls and downs the rest of his whiskey.

"You don't want to start that game with me, Reeves, because I don't want to take it off you, I want to rip it to pieces and I can't do that, can I? After all, I've made a promise. The middle door is the bathroom," he says and leaves me in the room by myself.

Completely caught off guard, I stride toward the bathroom and once I'm inside, I close the door behind me. I throw the T-shirt on the toilet seat and analyze myself in the mirror. I smile sadly when I realize how well put together, I look on the outside, my makeup still flawless and how broken I am on the inside.

How am I supposed to let my sister down like this when the entire reason I left the Phantoms in the first place was that Jess was starting to follow my example and fall into all kinds of wrong crowds?

I may be a hypocrite for not wanting her to turn out like me, but the people she was hanging with were ten times more dangerous than my crew. We were smart and careful; they were just high jocks.

I let out a deep breath and take off the dress, quickly hopping in the shower. I turn on the steaming hot water and let it soak my skin.

Why did I sleep with him? Why did I let myself so carried away and acted like a complete whore? Searching the shelf for something to wash myself with, I only find one bottle of shower gel, so I take it and open the lid. It smells like him. I cannot use this, it'd drive me insane, but I have nothing else with me. No clean clothes, and no clean underwear, so I have to use something to wash the sweat off, so I pour some in my palm and start rubbing it on my skin.

When I'm finished, I dry myself off with a clean towel, and put on the T-shirt which thank God is long enough to cover my underwear.

I exit the bathroom and head for the bedroom Brody indicated as being mine, relieved that he isn't anywhere to be seen.

How am I going to resist this guy when he lights up every nerve in my body and fills my head with all kinds of fantasies?

How should I resist him when my pussy throbs at the thought that he's two doors from me and I can bet his thoughts are just as dirty as mine?

I lay on the bed and when my head hits the pillow, a deep sigh escapes my lips. Although I was hoping that my mind would shut off and let me get some sleep, my head is filled with his voice, his breath and his touch. His big hands... How his big hands and those long fingers could satisfy me... My right hand reaches between my thighs involuntary, and I moan at the pleasure and shut my eyes.

I start rubbing my clit and move my fingers between my folds just I imagine he would before his tongue followed his fingers and a heavy sigh escapes my lips.

Imagining how Brody would look all ravished between my legs, I pick up my pace and I come

with breathy moans all over my own fingers.

***

It's 10 pm when I get back at Brody's apartment and not seeing him all day today has definitely helped me clear my head. I grabbed my stuff from my own apartment and took it all at Carter's Villa because I had nowhere else to leave it at.

When I open the apartment's door, I find Brody lost in thought on the sofa, his laptop on his lap with what looks like security footage of the apartment and surrounding area.

"Hi," he greets me, and I reply with the same

two letters.

All sweaty and gross, I decide I need a long steamy shower before I can order myself some food. I take the small bag of clothes in the bedroom and grab what I need for the shower.

When I leave the bathroom 20 minutes later, I am surprised to find Brody in the same spot, with a glass in his hand.

"I thought you might be sleeping," I whisper and swallow the lump in my throat while I stride toward the kitchen sink.

I am fully aware of Brody's gaze at my back as I walk past him, and I swear the hair on my arms rose at the attention. Traitor.

"You think I'd be able to sleep knowing you're in the shower next door? Completely naked, warm, and wet? he whispers low behind my ear, making me jump and my pulse quicken.

I don't know when he moved so fast and quietly, but now that his hands are on my waist, I don't think I care anymore.

He pulls me so close that I can feel his huge erection on my ass and all I want to do is grind on it. I close my eyes in the face of the feelings he's provoking me, blow out a deep breath, and tilt my head until it hits his chest. "Brody," I whisper a plea but I'm not sure what exactly I'm asking.

Do I want him to stop, or do I want him to continue?

"I know what you did last night. I could hear you through the bathroom wall," he says slowly and breathy and I swear that my body feels like it's on fucking fire. "Were you thinking of me when your fingers were doing what I'm supposed to do?"

I swallow and when his left hand trails a finger up my arm, I shudder. "Brody, please."

"Let me make love to you, Nina," he adds and slides my hair to one side so he can kiss my neck. He's driving me fucking crazy, but I can't do this, can I?

It's going to make things worse. I know it. He proved it to me.

"Brody we can't… we really shouldn't," I whisper and my breath hitches when his huge right hand roams down my belly, closer and closer to the spot that craves his attention the most, and my mind already paints an image that makes me moan louder.

His left hand touches the side of my breast and I forget how to breathe properly.

"We're way past what we should or shouldn't do. Let me show this body the attention it deserves," he whispers back, and I start moving my body without realizing it, hoping that his hand will reach the spot that's burning for him and when he does, sparks cloud my vision, and I don't want him to ever stop.

Brody's fingers reach under my panties, and I gasp at his touch. "You're so fucking wet for me, baby," the bastard smirks and inserts two long fingers inside me. I spread my legs further to give him full access and grab hold of his left arm to steady myself.

Brody growls and turns me around so quickly that I get lightheaded and have to grab hold of him with both hands. He rushes both hands at the sides of my face and smashes his lips onto mine with need and lust. I quickly find myself taking everything he has to offer with greed.

He then grabs my ass in his big hands and lifts me off the ground, "I need to feel you, now," he says with lust in his eyes and starts walking toward the counter, where he easily puts me down on the counter, spreads my legs wide and loses his pants in the blink of an eye, revealing the thick monster that I failed to notice on our last adventure, but definitely felt every inch it inside me. His eyes hold mine the entire time and I feel like I'm floating under his ocean gaze while he removes my t-shirt, leaving me completely bare in his arms, just as he is in mine.

Brody pulls my hips in one swift touch and pulls me to the edge of the counter, lines himself up with my wet entrance, and in one easy thrust, he buries himself deep inside of me, making me cry out in bliss. He stretches me up like no man has done before and I enjoy every inch of him with each delicious thrust.

With his hands gripping my hips hard, he fucks me with everything he has. "I promised you a bed," he whispers on my lips and pulls me up again, this time striding toward his bedroom, but he doesn't exit my throbbing pussy until we reach his bed, and he lays me down on my back.

Then he kneels before me, and I completely lose my mind when he parts my folds, inserts two fingers deep inside of me, and starts thrusting and curling them bringing me a type of pleasure that makes my face feel funny.

When his tongue slides between my folds though, that's when I lose it and start thrashing against the bed.

"Come for me, baby. I want you to come on my tongue," he demands with a growl, and it doesn't take long before I explode while his tongue continues its painfully delicious strides and his fingers keep thrusting me slowly, drawing out my orgasm.

When I bury my head on the bed, spent from what I just experienced, he removes his fingers, leaving me feeling empty, and what he does next leaves me fucking shocked. He takes his fingers in his mouth and sucks on them while his eyes hold mine captive.

Holly fuck, that was hot.

"Turn around" he orders in a lustful voice, and I do as I'm told, knowing this isn't over until he's fully satiated, not that I'm complaining.

I'm taken by surprise when I see myself on all fours in the massive mirror on top of his bed and when his massive, tattooed body comes behind my small frame, I watch it in awe and shock, completely amazed by how good we look together. He then spits in his palm, the move sending waves of pleasure through my body and after two slow pumps of his hand, he slides his cock back inside me and I feel full again.

Every thrust he makes builds up down my core into another earth-shattering orgasm. I can almost taste it on my tongue.

"Fuck, baby, your pretty pussy feels so good wrapped around my cock," he grunts behind me, and his fingers find my clit again, tracing right circles over it.

"Harder, Brody! I need you deeper," I moan and grind my ass to meet his thrusts, and that amplifies the pleasure ten times while his fingers work hard on my clit. I quickly feel my climax approaching like a tsunami and let myself ride it with noisy moans.

"Yeah, baby, say my name while you come," he grunts, and I do as I'm told.

"Oh God, Brody, yes, right there," I moan and almost fall on my face when the orgasm leaves me without any strength.

"Not God, just Brody. I'm your God," he growls and after a few more thrusts, he follows me into the sweet and delicious climax. "Now that I've got a taste, I'll never get enough of this sweet pussy, that's for sure," he adds when he collapses next to me, and I lay on my belly with a smile on my face.

There's another reason that should make me run, but I don't. I just lay there, looking at his beautiful face. "I should go get some sleep."

"You can stay if you want," he whispers and tucks a strand of hair behind my ear. This is seriously getting out of hand, and I need to go before whatever happens low in my belly, turns into more complicated things.

"I think it's best if I go, or this will never stop," I reply and cover my boobs because his lingering gaze makes my cheeks heat up.

Brody grabs the sheet and wraps it around his torso while sitting upright on the bed, with his back against the headboard. "None of us wants it to stop, so why do we have to stop it?"

"Because this job is dangerous and we can't get lost in each other, Brody," I say with a sad smile on my face. The attraction Brody and I have could be the best thing that's ever happened to me, and I want nothing more than to see where this could go,

"But we're so good together, Nina," he whines and kisses my bare shoulder.

"I'm sure you've had good sex before, Brody. It's best if we keep our distance when we don't have to work together. I'll stay in my room and try to avoid you as much as possible until I find a place to move."

I don't give Brody time to reply and head for the door. I grab his T-shirt from the kitchen, put it on, and run into the room I've been given, happy to find an empty, clean, and quiet bedroom.

I close the door behind me and stick my back to it, a smile growing on my face.

TEN | NINA

I wake up from all the light flooding the room but I'm still very tired. When I check the clock on my phone, I realize it's a bit after 7, which means I slept only 4 hours, because I remember how when I hit the pillow and checked my phone last night, it was 3 in the morning.

There's a message from Jess asking me why the doctor is telling her she's being moved to the Mayo Clinic, and I decide to make a quick coffee and go see her.

To my shock, I find Brody in the kitchen, making breakfast, so I head directly to the coffee machine without making a sound.

"See, I already don't like this. I don't want you to avoid me. I want us to be able to live together and work together. You don't have to move out," he speaks out and I have to turn around and face him. His eyes search my face for the answer, and I try to make sure I'm not as easy to read.

"Okay." It's all I say, and I can see that Brody's shocked by me agreeing so quickly.

It's not like I have another option. It feels like my life is falling apart more than usual.

"Okay then, breakfast?" He asks me and as much as I'd love something to eat, I have to go grab some clothes from my place before going to see Jess.

I bite the inside of my cheek and smile awkwardly. "I can't. I have somewhere I need to be."

"Okay, sure."

"I really have to go now; I'll see you later?"

"Here, have my keys. I'll be out most of the day, so you can get back in. I can ask Gettleman for another key if I need it, he lives 2 floors down," he explains and hands me his set of keys.

"Sure. Thank you," I say with a nod and after I run into the room to grab my phone, I walk out of the apartment.

***

When I reach the hospital a couple of hours later, freshly showered and dressed in one of my usual outfits, shorts, a crop top, and sneakers, I find myself hesitating before entering the huge building.

I know where to find my sister, but I still have to go to the reception to get my visitor pass, otherwise, I won't be able to get through security.

"Thanks, Bernice," I say to the nice lady at the desk and stride toward my sister's room, where I find her reading one of her steamy books. "Hey, sis," I greet her, and she smiles at me.

"Nina, where have you been? You disappeared

yesterday and never replied to my texts," she yells at me as soon as I close the door behind me. I knew this would come as soon as I saw all the texts last night but didn't reply to any of them.

"I'm sorry, I had a long night," I whisper with a heavy sigh and take a seat on the chair that's next to her bed.

"I can tell, you look like shit."

She laughs which means it was a joke, but I do feel like shit. Jess on the other hand looks ten times more tired than I do and that breaks my heart. Seeing her like this breaks my fucking heart.

"Oh, and here I was thinking I look flawless," I make a joke, hoping that she won't see right through my shit.

But she does. She sees right through it because she knows me better than anyone. "But you also look relaxed, did you get laid last night?" she adds a minute later, and I can't do anything but nod.

She knows me too well for me to try and lie my way out of this.

"I hate you and your instincts," I mumble and hit her arm playfully.

"Oh, come on, I'm just happy your coochie got some action, I hope he took good care of her, but now it's time to cut the crap and tell me why they're preparing to transport me to fucking Minnesota."

Here's the moment that scares the shit out of me.

Holding a gun, that's a piece of cake. Shooting someone in the face? Same. I love both of those things, but saying goodbye to my sister? That's fucking terrifying when cancer is involved, and tomorrow isn't promised.

"Because it's the best hospital in the country," I answer as seriously as possible.

"And it's all the way across the country. This hospital is in fifth place, so cut the crap. Tell me what's happening," she counters, putting me on the spot.

"Okay, fine. Here's the thing. Carter is going to take care of everything and pay for every treatment you need, with the condition that I send you to someplace far away and focus on the job."

Jess stares at me for a whole long minute before dropping her face in her palms and sighing deeply. "The job? Nina, no... please tell me you haven't agreed to any job..." she says after a few more minutes of silence.

"I can't do that because I did agree to a job. I need to do this, Jess. I can't help you in any other way and I'm sorry that you have to go through this alone, far from me. We're all we've got Jess and we have to beat this together even if we'll be a few miles apart. It's only for a month or two. I'll come get you before you know it and then we'll never have a care in the world again. I'm talking tens of millions, Jess," I try to sweeten the blow but I'm not sure it's working because her eyes become sad and worried in a second.

If she'll hate me for this, I'll be happy knowing that she's going to beat cancer and survive this. I'll be able to live with myself, when if I don't do everything in my power to make sure she gets to the other end of this, then I definitely will hate myself.

"I have a really bad feeling about this, Nina," she whispers with tears in her eyes.

I hold it together like a warrior when I reach to wipe her cheek, "I know, monkey face. It's not an easy job but you know us. We're a team and we have each other's backs, so we'll be fine. I promise."

"Promise me you'll send at least one text a day, so I know you're okay or I'll send the cops, Nina. I swear on my life I'll send the cops on Carter," she says with determination in her brown eyes, making me smile.

"I promise but the same goes for you. Now you go and beat the heck out of cancer," I say with a heavy heart when my phone pings in my pocket. I bring it out to check it, only to find a text from Carter, asking us to gather at his house. "I have to go now, beautiful, but remember that I'll be there even if you can't see me, monkey face. I'm always there with you."

I hug my sister tightly but don't linger too much or the tears that I hold in like a champion, will spill over and make me crumble at the foot of her bed. I wave goodbye with a heavy heart and exit the room to avoid seeing her in pain. Yes, I'm that much of a bitch because I'm afraid that if she asks me not to do this, I won't. I'd give up on everything if she asked me and right now, that means giving up on her life.

And that's not a fucking option!

ELEVEN | BRODY

When Nina finally joins us at Carter's house, I feel a weight lifting off my chest and I can't quite understand why I react like that. She salutes the crew with a nod and when I finally lock eyes with her, I smile uncontrollably but she quickly turns around, giving me a full view of the way those jeans she must've grabbed from her apartment, hug her perfectly round ass.

She's not a size 4 woman with boobs for her brain, she's probably a size 10 or 12, with long, thick legs, a bit of a belly, and nice breasts in a D cup by the looks of them.

"Nina, glad you could join us. Drink?" Carter greets her and he's already on his way to the bar to fetch her a drink.

"I'll take a water, thanks," Nina replies with an awkward smile.

Carter hands her the bottle of water a minute later, stands tall next to me, and proceeds to address the crew. "This is our last job. I need to make sure of that.

My age doesn't allow me to do this anymore and I want to do something different after this. Would it be legal? Probably not," he laughs. "You've been with me since you were 16, and for those who don't know that, that's 10 years ago, even if you left 2 years ago to get a fucking diploma," he shakes his head in disapproval.

I throw him a pointed look as if saying get to the fucking point already and lean on the bar completely bored and the others gather close by to hear what our friend here has to say. "Do you remember what I told you when you said you want out?"

"That you'll miss me?" She jokes and makes the others laugh.

Carter only smiles. "Yeah, not the point though. I said that you don't need a diploma to be a millionaire and I'm just about a month away from finally proving that to you."

Why do I feel like he schools her as if she's a back-row student about to repeat their grade? "Still don't see your point," the woman replies with a raised brow that puts a dumb smile on my face.

"What I'm trying to say is that you're fucking brilliant, woman. You're the smartest woman I've ever met, and you don't need a fucking degree. You just need the proper tools. This job wouldn't be possible without you and your Romanian roots, because for the first part, you're essential and that means that whatever you want, goes. So, here's the thing, to afford all the equipment we need to steal those cars, we need a budget that we don't have and to get that kind of money, we're going to steal a very expensive necklace."

Now, this just got interesting. "Diamonds?" she asks with a tiny smile in the corner of her mouth and sparkles in her eyes.

"Not any diamonds, Red Scarlet, a necklace by James Currens that's worth 15 million dollars. Currens has a promotional contract with Miss World, and all the girls qualified will wear the necklace for an interview," he explains, and I find myself shaking my head.

I'm starting not to like this one bit. Everything being on her shoulders for the first part of the job doesn't sit well with me.

If she gets caught, we'll never finish the job, which means I won't get what I need.

Nina points at Carter before speaking out, "I've never heard of this man in my life, but I do know a thing or two about Miss World to know that you have had to have been a winner in your own country to qualify, and I've never won."

"You haven't, but Diana Munteanu did, and she's received a hefty payment so that you can use her name." He claps his hands and says with excitement.

"Damn, Carter. This might be your best work so far," interrupts the one named Jaxon, who's been sitting silently in the corner watching us closely.

"Let's say we got in, she wears the shiny thing and we do get away with stealing it, then what? How do we disappear, where do we sell it?" I ask too many questions which I know for a fact that annoys the shit out of Carter.

I have to though. Everything sits on these jobs, and they have to end up perfectly for us to walk away from it. It also means we need 10 backup plans.

"We'll sell it on the black market in New Mexico and then proceed our way toward Colorado. But don't sweat it, Brody, because the copy I'm having a very good replicator work on for two years, will cover for us so we can get out of the state and maybe even finish the job. It'll cover for us long enough to be able to disappear before they uncover everything."

"It sounds like you've thought of every detail, Carter, and that worries me," Simon makes a joke and instinctively my eyes search Nina's, who smiles like a sorority girl, and that only makes my body tense.

Carter chuckles and points a finger at Nina with a cheeky smile on his face, "I did, now I only need to find out if you speak any Romanian, and if you don't, this might all go to shit."

She only frowns in confusion. "I do. I mean I used to until my mom passed, but I'm not sure I'm still good at it."

He claps his hands loudly and looks at her with bewildered eyes, scaring me for a second. We all watch him in confusion because we don't understand much. "That's okay, that's good because that means that bringing Diana's manager from Romania wasn't a complete waste of time."

"It looks like you thought this through, Carter and that worries me. It's usually the best plans that go to shit first," I say with a head shake.

Something doesn't sit right with me.

"Not this one, my man. I've been waiting for the Red Scarlet for a couple of years now and have made a tight plan of how to steal it. I promise you; it has no flaws."

Nina though, is just as concerned as I am. "Why did you have to complicate things, Carter? I thought we only needed to steal the cars, but now you want a double job in the span of a few weeks? That's dangerous."

"It's not complicated at all. I promise you. This part is like a pre-game," Carter assures us and raises his glass, waiting for us to do the same.

"I made a copy," she hands me my set of keys, which attracts Levi's unwanted attention, and he looks way more pissed than he should.

"You two live together? What the fuck?" He growls and takes a few strides toward Nina, so I frown and raise a brow, waiting for an explanation of why that would ever be his fucking problem.

"What's your problem, pretty boy? Need your face fixed?" I take a step toward the male, and I clench my jaw so hard I'm afraid it might snap from the force. If I didn't like him before, now I definitely despise his ass.

I hear Nina sigh and see her drag a hand across her face. "Hey, knock it off, both of you!" She shouts at us in annoyance but that only makes me hard.

She's so fucking hot when she's all bossy and irritated.

"You're my problem. You think you can come in here and do whatever you want?" Levi shouts all in my face and I show him a wicked smile before I throw a perfectly balanced punch and make him bleed and wobble back a few steps.

"I thought you don't fuck teammates," he bites back and grabs Nina's arm with a grip that looks painful, and that only makes me lose my mind even further.

"Did you just dare to fucking touch her," I growl like a fucking animal on the brick of going feral. I yank the fucker away from Nina and throw him on the ground, then charge at him with a newfound rage. "I'll rip your fucking arms off and feed them to you if you lay one finger on her again."

I punch him repeatedly until I hear his skull crack under my fist and Carter has to drag me off him. "This has to end, now! I can't have you mess this up. Any of you!"

I'm completely shocked and turned on when all of a sudden, Nina brushes past me like a storm and punches the bastard that just managed to get up. "Now it can end. Touch me one more time, Levi, and I swear I'll kill you myself."

"That is no way for a lady to behave," we're distracted by a woman's voice and when I turn my attention toward her, I find a tall, skinny redhead walking slowly toward us. She smiles and hugs Carter first.

"Everyone, this is Christina Dumitrescu, coming all the way from Romania."

Should I be impressed by that? I'm not and neither is Nina, who looks the woman up and down in annoyance because of her earlier comment.

"Tu trebuie să fii Nina," the woman addresses the brunette on my left with a smirk on her face.

"I am," it's all she says.

"Brody Mason," I introduce myself briefly when she locks eyes with me and throws me a dashing smile that makes Nina snort.

The woman sizes me up and down and lingers on my crotch which seems to be forever hard when around Nina. "Pleasure to meet you, handsome."

I chuckle low and wink at her. "I suggest you keep it moving or she'll rip out your throat out."

"Are you two together?"

"Nope," I reply with a laugh.

"Nina, văd că înțelegi ce spun, dar refuzi să-mi vorbești," she speaks the same language that I assume is Romanian because Nina seems to understand it.

"You are correct," Nina replies to whatever Christina said to her in her language.

"Listen, babe, if we want to work together, this attitude has to go." She lingers in front of Nina and works her fingers through the brunette's hair.

Even I know that was a bad idea.

"Firstly, I am not your babe, and secondly, this attitude means I don't like you. I don't have to like you to work with you. Now take a step back before I crack your nose open."

Fuck man. I can't walk around with a full-on erection in my fucking pants and that's what she does to me.

Christina raises a brow and clenches her jaw but doesn't move an inch, so Carter intervenes before we see one more bloodied nose. "It's quite late so what do you ladies say if you meet tomorrow for coffee to release some of this tension?"

"Usually, I release the tension with sex, you up for that?"

Nina laughs out loud with shaking shoulders, but I can't say if she actually liked Christina's joke or is just sarcastic. "I'm out of here."

She stalks toward the door, and I watch her every move.

I fucking love that ass and I just realized that I need to see it bounce off my dick tonight.

TWELVE | NINA

I'm surprised that when I stop at a red traffic light on my way to Brody's apartment, he stops right next to me. I smile without realizing it and he waves and mouths something that takes me a second to understand. "Up for another race?"

I laugh out loud, "Not today, amigo. I can't see straight, that's how hungry I am."

"Go home, I'll grab something for us to eat. Favorites?"

"Udon Noodles," I reply and with a nod, and he shoots off because it's green now.

I smile like an idiot the entire way home and when I get to the apartment and sink into the sofa, I can swear that it feels like home.

A lot cozier than it should.

I check my phone quickly for any texts from my sister, and I find one saying she's been put on a flight as soon as I leave because everything's been paid for.

So, Carter kept his word, or at least some of it. I reply to her text and when I want to say something about the landlord selling the apartment, I remember that I haven't told her about that, so I keep it that way.

Until she comes back happy and healthy, there's no need for her to know that we don't have a home for now. She'll just worry about where I sleep and that'll just bring more questions.

I tell her to rest and that I love her before putting the phone away.

It's not that long before Brody strolls in with heavenly-smelling food. I don't think I've ever been so happy to see a man in my life. "That smells like heaven, did you grow wings?"

"No, but Beijing House might've."

I laugh.

Brody puts the food boxes on the coffee table and sits down next to me, making me suddenly aware of his overwhelming presence.

We eat, we turn on friends and laugh with our mouths full and we get cozy.

Too cozy.

"What's wrong? Is it the food?" Brody asks, concern filling his voice.

"No. The food is perfect, this... is too perfect," I whisper in sadness. "Who are we trying to fool, Brody? Can we honestly give us a real shot amid this madness that we're trying to pull?"

Brody averts his gaze, and I can see his jaw tic.

"I can't fall for you, Brody. I can't afford that."

I swallow the lump in my throat and put the food down, suddenly losing my appetite.

"You're right, you can't fall for me Nina, because I won't be able to love you the way you deserve to be loved and I'd hate to see you hurt because of me." I don't realize that the stress and overwhelming feelings that accumulated for the past 24 hours are now spilling over my cheeks. "I loved once with every fiber in my being, and when I lost that person, everything went with her."

I continue to cry without making a sound. I cry for his loss. I cry for the woman he lost, and I cry for me. For what builds up in my heart but can't let it grow.

"Please don't cry, I shouldn't have said anything, bella," he reaches to wipe my tears with his thumb, and I find it hard to breathe.

I take a long steadying breath before I manage to speak again. "I can't stay here."

"I know, baby. It's okay. You're an extraordinary woman, Nina. Probably one in a million and I'm a fool to let you go, but I can't give you what you need and deserve."

I've known this man for less than a week, so why am I heartbroken to hear him say this?

Why does it affect me so much, when I know we'd never work out anyways?

I take a deep breath in to regain my calm.

"I'll take this to the room; hope you don't mind."

"Whatever makes you comfortable," he agrees, and I leave with a nod.

I need to be by myself for a bit to regain my focus and to put to sleep whatever happens in my belly when I'm around Brody.

Hiding in the comfort of my room, I take

a deep breath and pull out my phone to call Carter. He's the only option I have left. *"Reeves, everything okay?"*

"Carter, hi. Yeah, all's good. I need a favor though. Can I stay at your apartment downtown until we run off?"

"Of course, you can, but Christina lives there too. She didn't want to stay with me at the villa. If you can share that without killing each other, then you're more than welcome to stay there."

"I'll try," I breathe out.

Carter chuckles. *"Good, I'll let her know."*

He hangs up and I put the phone on my nightstand but then grab it back to search for something that's been on my mind for a very long time. I open my unused Facebook page and search for the name I got out of my mom a long time ago. David Bloomberg, my birth father.

I was five when he left us and Mom had just given birth to Jess when he realized that this, two children and a housewife wasn't what he wanted and left us to take care of ourselves. I was too young to understand what happened and I missed him and would blame Mom for a very long time before I got older and understood how things were.

That he wasn't man enough to take care of his family and bailed on us.

I find a few in L.A. but can't seem to be attracted by any of them in particular. There are 2 in New York, one in Canada, and one in

Colorado. I become more interested in the one in Colorado because I know I'll go there soon, but when I open his profile, I find the male version of Jessica and I gasp out loud.

I try to contain my rage and scroll through his profile, hoping to find an old man living a low life, but what I find is far from that. David Bloomberg is living his best life with his 2 kids and blonde wife in the upper side of Cherry Hills Village, which is the richest town in the whole fucking country, and judging by the boy's pictures, they look a couple of years younger than Jess, which means they're in their twenties.

Motherfucker!

With a clenched jaw, I can't hold it in anymore and I smash the phone onto the wall in front of me with a frustrated scream.

Of course, I completely forgot Brody was in the living room until he comes running in. "Are you okay?"

"I am. My phone, not so much." I pick up my phone and look at the cracked screen. When I try to turn it on, it lights up so that must mean it works. "Would you look at that, it survived."

"Who pissed you off?"

"The face of a dick."

"An ex-boyfriend?"

"Yes, but not mine though," I joke and start laughing out loud. "My mom's."

It doesn't take long before Brody relaxes and joins me with an honest laugh. "Why does your mom's ex bother you?"

"Because 20-something years ago he decided he didn't want to deal with 2 children and a housewife and left us, but now he's got a perfect little family."

Damn, it feels really good to voice that.

"What a douche. Wanna hunt him down?"

I smile. "I probably will after this."

"You have a sibling?"

"I do. I have a younger sister. She's the reason I'm doing this again."

He smiles back but the smile doesn't reach his blue eyes. "We all have our reasons for doing this."

"What's yours?" I ask.

"If I'd tell you I'd have to kill you, and I've grown to like you."

"Good night, Brody," I say with a smile on my face and climb back in my bed, hoping he'll let me go to sleep, this time without any events.

He waves and closes the door behind him, leaving me alone once more.

THIRTEEN | NINA

I stand in front of Carter's apartment, suitcase in hand, unsure if I should or shouldn't knock on the brown door. Do I want to deal with Christina's face so quickly? Probably not, but I don't have a choice, so I knock three times.

When the door opens, I feel like I'm going to throw up in her stupid smug face. "Oh, look what the cat dragged in. You lost? Otherwise, I can't imagine why you'd come to my door."

I clench my jaw and my fists, trying very hard not to punch her and ruin her perfect makeup. "Good thing is not your door then."

This woman is truly impossible.

I storm past her into the living room and hear her chuckle behind me as she strolls to the couch. "You have some temperament problems, sweetheart."

"I don't have time for this, Christina. You know we'll live together for a while, so cut the crap and stay out of my sight." I simply say and go toward the kitchen to grab a glass of water. Good thing I've lived here before and know my way around.

"I have to admit, you have balls to want to live with me. I could kill you in your sleep," she says in all seriousness and crosses her arms over her chest.

I laugh. "Listen, Christina, honestly, I've got nothing against you. I don't have the time to hate you, so here's how we're going to do this. We'll work on my Romanian, and you'll help me learn more about the country, in case I need it. Again, I won't pretend to like you in the process. You're here to do a job, just like me, but try not to piss me off while you do it."

Am I a mean girl?

Sometimes I can be. I never let killing people affect me. I do it for my own gain and I'm pretty sure that makes me a villain, and will definitely not land me in heaven, but I don't slack at my job. I don't blow a job just because I don't like someone. I'm damn good at being professional, and I hope she is too.

"Look, Nina. I'll tell you what. I see that you are the only woman on the crew and I'm not here to change that. I'm a temporary thing because I'll be out of here so fast, you'll ask yourselves if I was ever even real." Her words make me laugh.

"Wise words. I didn't peg you to be the type."

"Don't be fooled by how I act around men. Where I come from, it's the norm," she replies with a sad smile.

I frown. "I was always curious about my mom's roots, but I think now I understand why my grandparents sent her away. How did you end up knowing Stark?"

Christina sighs before replying. "I could ask

you the same thing." Smart woman, but I'm smarter. We're not quite there yet.

"Long story. How do I win this thing, Christina? That's important. I can bet that we both have someone important relying on this job."

The red-haired woman nods. "The most important thing at Miss World besides beauty, are skills and hobbies. Carter told me that you're quite good with guns and stealing things. Think of these two things as an art, add a sob story and we're in the final."

I process it all and nod slowly lost in thought.

I might be able to pull this whole thing off. "Will they even care about the language?"

"I'll be completely honest with you, even though we haven't started on a very pretty note. I'm pretty sure they couldn't care less, but when Carter reached out to buy Diana out, I saw it as an opportunity.

I need this job more than air, Nina, so I did everything in my power to get here, even if it meant sucking dick and saying a few lies along the way." I completely understand.

I'm in no position to judge Christina when I'm up to doing anything for the money that pays to save my sister's life.

"Do we know when the pre-selection is?" I ask.

"In 2 days, so even if we wanted to do anything about the language, 2 days isn't enough time, not when you have a full head of problems.

Which you seem to have because otherwise, you wouldn't be here."

"You have no idea," I blow out a deep breath.

When did we become friends?

FOURTEEN | BRODY

The day of the pre-selection came way quicker than anyone had expected but we are all hoping that what the girls had prepared was enough to get us through this.

I'm in the hotel lobby, waiting for Nina and Christina when a blond girl with a Miss Colombia banner doesn't stop looking at me. She's tall and definitely beautiful, one of the reasons she's here in the first place, but Nina's smile comes to mind, and I shake my head. This girl looks like she's not older than 20, and I don't do sorority girls anymore. I'm at an age where I'm barely attracted to women under 30, Nina being the exception, regardless of how pretty or hot they are.

"Hi handsome, are you competing?" She asks with a purr, but my eyes are locked on the brunette whose curves I'm beginning to know.

Nina strolls into the hotel lobby and I become fully aware of the entire room's eyes being on her and I suddenly want to commit murder, because the way her damn dress hugs her body plays a dangerous game with my mind.

The slit on her right leg makes my mouth go dry, and I find myself using my tongue to moisten my lips. I won't even look at her cleavage because I might take her right here in the middle of the hotel and I already want to rip out the eyes of every fucker who now drools and stare at her from each side because the hotel is full of just as many men as women.

I quickly find myself growling at the nearest one to me. "This is your one chance to look away or I'll rip your fucking eyeballs from your skull and feed them to you."

The man quickly turns away and disappears behind a door. Nina, however, gives me a wide sincere smile. "It looks like you like what you're seeing."

"I'm not the only one though and I feel my patience slipping away," I reply with a clenched jaw.

"Tsk, Tsk, we're not doing this, Brody. Let's get this over with."

"You're playing with my soul, Reeves. You've got no mercy, woman?" I whisper shout and take a step closer to her. "You realize that someone has to take care of this." I grab her hand and pull it down to my crotch so she can feel what she's doing to me.

"I hope she bites," she spits at me and turns on her heel toward Christina, asking for a cigarette.

With blood boiling in my veins, I turn around and start searching for the Colombian blond woman, whom I find very quickly and gesture her toward the nearest bathroom. I smile when I see her heading toward it and I make my way there a second behind her.

When I open the door, I find her ready on the sink and after I close the door behind me, I assault her lips with need. However, I can't stop my mind from going back to when I had taken Nina for the first time, in a bathroom. "I need you inside me, now!" she demands but I stop in my tracks.

I can't even fuck another woman, that's how much the brunette fucks my head.

I look the woman in the surprised eyes for a second and then proceed to exit the bathroom and run toward the back exit, where I know Nina went to smoke. I had no fucking idea she smoked.

"Don't lose your head for him, Nina. He's not worth it," I hear Christina before I come into their view and stay around the corner just a bit more. I'm curious what she'll say because it's damn obvious they're talking about me.

Nina laughs in frustration. "He exasperates me, Chris. One second, he wants me, the next he shoves me away, then he's jealous and wants to bone me. I feel used every time he touches me and I feel like I'm losing my mind."

I feel like struck by lightning, rooted on the spot by every word she says. I couldn't use her even if I wanted to.

"The first time we met and locked eyes, almost a week ago, although it feels like a lifetime since, I felt butterflies in my belly. Fucking butterflies. Now I almost despise him for what he's doing to me without even realizing it."

I back away and get back inside the building. I can't stomach the rest of that conversation, and I've heard enough as it is. I told her I didn't want her to suffer because of me, but here I am, making her suffer.

I need to control myself. I need to take back control because I'm not like this.

Clenching my jaw, I take the earpiece out of my pocket and place it in my ear. "Can you guys hear me?"

"Affirmative."

"The parking lot is filled with cameras at each pillar, we can't use that. We need a getaway car on the street, not the underground. Two guys at the lift down there too."

"How many cameras are inside the hotel?"

"We're still in the lobby where there's too many of them, but I have an idea," I say as soon as I see the catering team car pulling up outside. "The event has its own catering agency, so that might help us more than you think. I just have to see the event floor before I think of anything."

Nina and Christina quickly come into view and after a court nod, all three of us head upstairs to the fifth floor to start the show.

The silence is deafening, and the tension is tangible in the elevator as we go up. None of us look at one another and we all find something else to focus on. When the lift doors open, I swear I can hear the brunette sigh in relief.

We're greeted by a lady with a clipboard and Nina remembers to use the girl's name with an accent. "Diana Munteanu, Romania."

The woman smiles at us and hands each one of us a name tag that only says visitor or contestant on it and disappears. The room is packed with women from all the countries that I guess have qualified and their staff.

I have to say, I'm not sure I love all the attention I'm suddenly getting. Usually when my tattoos are more visible if I keep a stone face, they don't stare for too long, but dressed in a suit that hugs every muscle and with only my finger tattoos visible, that defense is out the window, and from how Nina looks at each one of them, I fear for their lives. "Relax, bella, I can read the thirst for killing in your eyes."

"Nope, this is my friendly face. You can take them one by one if you want," she shrugs, and I find myself not liking her cheerful tone, but I hide my displease with a mischievous grin.

I'm aware I'm not some Greek god, and I'm not some romantic sweet soul, but I do know how to please a woman in bed. That means that I know that she's craving my dick as much as I crave her pussy and I won't rest until I'll have her admit it.

Fuck this, it's obvious we can't stay away from each other or let other people near one another, so why suffer? I can't wait to have her bouncing off my dick later tonight.

"This scares me more than death, I hate it," she

adds, meaning the entire competition thing. I'd hate it too if I were her.

I snort. "Death shouldn't scare you, sweetheart, but what dies inside us while we're alive, that's the sad part."

I shouldn't have said that but it's true. When we lose someone, a part of ourselves goes with them and I lost too many people to be able to bear more.

"Funny of you to say that, when I'm pretty sure you killed your own heart so that you'd not feel any pain," she bites back and I'm quite surprised by her outburst.

She's not wrong though. "It's not any type of pain, and until you go through it, you won't understand."

"You have no idea in how many ways I know pain, Brody Mason, so don't you dare talk to me like I'm a protected princess. Looks like I'm next," she barks at me and strolls to the line-up.

There she goes, being right again. I know nothing about this woman but in all fairness, I've only known her for a few days even if it feels like I've known her for years.

It's not long before she gets on the stage and starts addressing the crowd like she's doing this every day.

"Good evening, my name is Diana Munteanu, and I'm coming from Romania," even though I can hear her in the event's speakers, I can also hear her in my ear, because she hasn't turned off her earpiece. She starts pacing the stage from left to right, which could mean that she's nervous, but she's so composed that even I can't be sure.

I burst out laughing when Nina jumps off the stage with the grace of a swan and walks slowly toward the judges' table. She places both palms on top of their table and leans forward, targeting one of the men at that desk. This all worked out perfectly with the panel being all men. I watch her face closely as she studies the man for a brief second before continuing her speech. "You see, it's not easy to be an orphan back there and that pushes most of us to learn to survive."

That being said, she turns around with a smile on her face and jumps back on the stage. A second later she brings up her right hand, holding a wallet, but not any wallet, one of the judge's wallet.

Everyone started to whisper because just like me, they probably never saw her picking it up.

Damn, she's good.

"Many will argue that regardless of the reason, stealing is still a crime, but Robin Hood wasn't a criminal, right? He was a vigilante, he was helping the ones in need, well I wish I didn't have to say this, but I was feeding dozens of children with what I managed to steal and if that makes me a criminal, you can throw me in jail. Thank you." she ends her piece and I'm left watching her and wondering if any of it was true, but I'm pretty sure she grew up in America, so I guess that's my answer.

We have to stick around until every contestant has been presented, so I head for the bar with the remaining time we have left, although there are just about 5 girls in the cue. Nina and Christina, who's always been beside me, follow suit and we all sit in silence at the bar. I order myself a whiskey on the rocks and the ladies both grab a martini.

"I have to say, I'm impressed. I believed every word you said," Christina raises her glass to toast for this small win. Nina does the same with a smile and takes a big sip out of it.

Step one was complete and now we have to proceed with caution.

This mini job with the necklace could always turn out to be more trouble than it's worth.

I've known Carter for years and always treated him like family, although he wanted nothing to do with my world and the gun trafficking, we remained friends throughout the years, and now when I needed him the most, he not only offered me shelter, but he also offered me an opportunity to disappear and have the means to never look back again.

First, we have to steal these things, and then make sure we won't get caught.

The Phantoms have been operating for 10 years and they always managed to slip through police's hands.

I am much safer with them than I ever was

with the Masoni's.

FIFTEEN | NINA

Brody watches closely every move I make and every sip of the drink I take. Every time I look his way, his gaze lands on mine instantly and my body heats up like a torch.

All the other contestants have left hours ago and so has Christina, but here we are, meters apart like we are strangers, drowning our sorrows in alcohol.

When a man takes away my focus from Brody when he sits between us, I frown with displease, but quickly realize that he's one of the judges and has just ordered me a drink. "Richard Stevens, a pleasure to meet you, Miss Munteanu."

The man kisses my hand like a gentleman, and I can swear I heard Brody growl like a feral animal behind him. "You've done a very good job up there, you're definitely up for running," he adds with a cheeky smile.

Up for running. What does that even mean?

His green eyes search my face for anything, but I can't tell he can't read me and that doesn't make him very happy. Richard is the type of rich man who owns women, unlike Brody, who venerates women. "This is all very exciting, Mr. Stevens." I play my part and that's being a very cheery girl from Romania who's in America for the first time.

His smile grows wider. "Oh, call me Richard."

"It's nice to meet you too, Richard." I purr and inch closer, suddenly understanding what he implies and what he wants.

Pleased with my answer, he quickly places a palm on my thigh and leans forward a bit. "I'll leave you my hotel room key, in case you want to make sure you're qualified." He places a key card in my palm and proceeds to walk away.

Richard isn't ugly or old, he is just ballsy and that is okay.

It's exactly what you want in a man, right?

I get off the bar stool ready to go seal the deal when Brody jumps from his own chair and grabs my arm with anger. "We're busy, we don't have time for you to get fucked. Let's go."

Maybe I wouldn't even have gotten through with this plan, but he just made sure I do anything to puss him off even more because no man will ever tell me what to do.

I made sure of that when I became independent at 16 years old.

I clench my teeth and break free from his hold. "Fuck you," I bark and turn around to leave.

"Nina, I swear on my life that if you don't come out with me, I'll cut him up in little pieces and deliver it to you at breakfast," he threatens me with a furious tone but that won't stop me because even he can't be that crazy.

We're not even a couple, we're nothing to each

other and if after two fucks he thinks I'm his property, I'll prove him the opposite.

A sudden thrill ran down my spine as I walk into the elevator, and I smile in excitement.

I went from not fucking at all to fucking more than one man in a few days and I don't know how I feel about that, but there's sure some kind of thrill to the idea of being pleased by a stranger. Maybe that's why I enjoy sex with Brody so much because he is a complete stranger.

When I reach Richard's hotel room, number 416, I use the key card to let myself in but only to find a completely empty room. I shrug and throw my purse on the bed, I'm sure he'll show up at some point.

I call room service and ask them to send up some champagne of ice, some wine and some croissants because it sounds like I'm starving.

The nature of my job can't let me get something out of this situation and I find myself snooping through Richard's stuff, hoping to find something that I could use later if this doesn't work out. However, it isn't long before there's a knock on the door and I open it excited for the room service, it's obvious that Richard has a spare key card.

Too bad it isn't room service greeting her at the door, but a very angry Brody. He pushes the door to the wall and grabs me by the throat in a gesture that should terrify me, but it doesn't. Fuck, it ignites a fire low in my belly and I swallow hard. "You want to be fucked, Reeves? Is that what you need? A long sweaty fuck that makes your legs hurt afterward? I'll fuck you, baby. I'll fuck you so good you won't even remember your name."

"Brody," I manage to whisper and stagger back so he can close the door. God forbid Richard shows up now and our plan would end so much sooner.

"He'll never make you feel the way I make you feel, understand?" He grits out and throws me on the bed.

This should scandalize me, but my body doesn't seem to catch up with my mind. It reacts to him in unhealthy ways. Brody starts unbuckling his belt and for the first time tonight, I see him in his true beauty.

Damn it, he's ravishing in this black tux, so he could have any damn woman in this hotel and yet, he's here with me.

I open my mouth to argue with him, but I don't get that far because we both hear the key card and the door being unlocked. "In the closet, now Mason! Don't you dare make a sound."

With a snarl, Brody listens to my pleas and makes himself small in the closet, so I close the double doors squeezing him in.

Let's be clear, he's a massive man and the closet wouldn't even fit me, but somehow, we manage.

Richard approaches the bed with steady steps and when he sees me, he smiles broadly. "Now this is a nice surprise. I have to admit, Miss Reeves, I didn't think you'd accept my proposal."

I chuckle and stand tall in front of him. "I think it's time you call me Nina. After all, your head will be between my legs." I grab his tie and loosen it up while his stare takes my face in.

"Depends on which head," he replies with an arrogant grin.

"Both, darling," I say with a charming smile.

"I knew why I picked you," he replies.

I swallow the lump in my throat and show him an awkward smile. As much as I'd like to put on a show for Brody and make him pay for the way he's treating me, I'm afraid of how he'll react to what he sees because I'm sure as hell he won't be able to stay put.

Richard loses his suit jacket and starts undoing his shirt one button at a time, while his gaze doesn't leave mine. He quickly starts unbuckling his belt and draws out his fully erect cock with his right hand.

The sight of it doesn't do anything for me but when his left-hand reaches for the back of my head, takes a good handful of my hair, and starts pulling me down toward his dick, that's when I want to punch him in the guts.

I don't get too close to his dick though because in the next second a pop rings in the room and Richard's blood splatters on my face and although warm, it feels like a bucket of iced water. "Oh my God, what did you do?" I whisper and wipe my eyes clean.

"You're playing with me, Reeves," he whispers and takes a step toward me. "Or maybe you like being treated like that?" He gestures toward Richard's body, now lying at my feet, and takes another step, making my heartbeat faster and a lump forming in my throat. "You want me to grab you by the hair?" He adds and after one more step, he's inches away from me and I have to tilt my head a little to keep eye contact.

"Brody..." I manage to choke out just as his hand flies in my hair and I feel like a trapped mouse. "You're mine, Reeves. Do you understand? You're all I can think about and the thought of you with someone else makes my blood boil. So you're mine, baby. Mine to kiss," he whispers and places a soft kiss on my lips.

"Mine to touch," he adds and reaches my throbbing pussy with his right hand over my silky dress. "Mine to have," he continues to rub my clit over the thin fabric. "And mine to..." but he never finishes. He never says what I need to hear in order to be his.

Like awoken from a deep sleep, I sigh deeply and push him away with all my strength. "No! We promised we're not doing this, Brody. I'm done here, clean up this mess."

I walk away from him and damn, it feels good.

He quickly became my weakness like no other man was ever able to get under my skin like this.

SIXTEEN | NINA

I open my eyes slowly and get out of bed in one quick motion. I know that lingering will only make it harder to get up so I head for a strong coffee. I need the biggest mug in the kitchen to deal with the migraine I seem to have.

When I exit the room, the doorbell rings twice, so I head toward the door to see who's visiting so early, but only to find a box and a bouquet of white roses, but no one else in sight. Shrugging I pick up the flowers and the box and head back inside. I drop the box on the dining table when Christina comes out of her own room. "Who's that from?"

"Brody," I whisper after I read the card that came with the flowers. *A promise is meant to be held.*

"Do I want to know what's inside that?" she whispers and gets two mugs from the kitchen to pour us some coffee.

I shake my head and take a deep breath before I open the box. "No, you don't," I whisper just as I quickly close it back. A promise is meant to be kept, but this is the one he keeps? This man is fucking nuts because in that box, I'm pretty sure I was staring at Richard's fingers and tongue.

"He wants to play? I'll play," I mumble and head to the kitchen counter, box in hand. "Christina, you might wanna go before you lose your appetite."

She doesn't argue with me and only lifts her left eyebrow in question. "It's best you don't know."

"I'm going to take this in bed, then," she replies and leaves the kitchen.

I go back to my room to grab my phone and give the perpetrator a quick call. When he doesn't pick up, I leave him a voice mail I hope he'll listen to. *'Brody, thanks for the flowers. I want to apologize for last night. I really want us to get along, so I'm making lunch. Come over.'*

After I hung up the phone, I start working on lunch as promised. This lunch has to be one he'll remember forever.

***

Time flies and the doorbell rings suddenly. I do smile though, because everything is ready. "Brody, happy you got my message. Come on in," I gesture toward the table and he enters the apartment with a smug smile on his stupid, handsome face.

What surprises me more than anything is that I'm seeing him for the first time dressed like a normal person. No boots or leather jacket. Today he's wearing black jeans with a grey t-shirt that hugs his body in ungodly ways that make me stare. His arms are all free of cover and I can finally admire his tattooed sleeves. They're so fucking beautiful that I could orgasm just touching them.

"I have to say, after what I sent you this morning, I wasn't expecting you to be so friendly," he replies with a confused look on his face and sits at the table.

"How did you know I like roses?" I ask and smile like a schoolgirl.

"I guessed. Did you get the box?"

"What box?" I frown and continue to fill the plates with soup and carry them to the table.

I sit across from Brody and wait for him to say something about the box. "I dropped off a box with the roses. You didn't find it?" He asks while his gaze searches my face for any sign of a lie. He smells something, but that's not enough to ruin my plan.

"No. No box. I just woke up and I'm starving, let's eat first."

He nods and grabs the spoon, taking the first bite. "I didn't know you were cooking. This is really good. What meat is this?" he adds while taking a huge bite of the bony piece of meat.

"I'm not doing it often. I'm glad you like it; it's been cooked with a lot of fingers." I take a long pause before saying the last word and wait for his reaction with a mischievous smile.

Brody frowns for a few seconds before his face completely turns into a terrified look and runs to the bathroom so fast that I barely see him.

He doesn't know where the bathroom is, so first he opens Christina's door and she shouts at him, then he opens the one leading to the bathroom.

I get up from the table and walk slowly toward him, just to watch him retching like a sorority girl after a party. "Nina, please tell me you're joking. Please, woman, I beg you."

I have to admit that seeing this huge man in my bathroom, crumbling on a toilet is funny and weird.

"It's good to know that this scares you, but yes. It was pig's tails, not Richard's fingers. I hope this will teach that next time you do something like this, Mafia bullshit, I will feed you their balls."

"You're crazier than I thought," he chokes out a laugh and wipes at his mouth.

"You're the one to talk when you mailed me 10 digits," I reply and throw him a bottle of ice-cold water. I know that'll help the burn of his throat.

Now that he feels better, he's more like himself and honestly, I'm glad.

"I think you just might be made for me," he whispers and wraps me in his arms in a gesture that makes me freeze in his embrace.

"You have to go, Brody," I reply with a sigh and take a step back. I can't do this without getting involved and he doesn't want to get involved. He made that clear when he said he couldn't love me back.

"You're right. I'll see you later at Carter's."

We don't say anything else; he lingers for a moment searching my face like he's trying to memorize it and then leaves before I can speak again.

When I return to the kitchen, I find Christina cutting some vegetables for a salad, completely lost in her thoughts. "How far lost are you?"

"Too far for a definite number. I wish you never knew this painful separation," she replies with a sigh and a sad smile.

"And what if I do? Any advice on how to survive it?" I laugh and grab a bar stool to sit on and an apple from the basket.

Christina stops cutting the vegetables for a second and looks me in the eye. "If there's an easier way not to miss someone, I didn't find it yet. It can't be a man you're far away from, because what you have with this guy doesn't happen when you're involved with someone else, so who is it?"

"That obvious, huh?" I ask and take a big bite of the green fruit.

"You kidding, right? The tension is always palpable with you two."

"It's my sister, I had to send her across the country for her cancer treatments to be able to focus on this job. You?" I share with the complete stranger that I met less than a week ago but feel completely comfortable with.

"My baby. I have a 5-year-old daughter, Elena and she's been diagnosed with multiple sclerosis 10 months ago. I've been trying to get her the right treatments ever since and now I can. I'm only helping until we get the necklace and I'll be gone before you know it," she says like a warning not to get attached to a friendship that can't last and it makes me think about Brody too.

How I can't get attached to him when I know that I will always put my sister first and will do what's best for her. How I know nothing about him, and he knows nothing about me, yet my heart flutters every time I see him, and I wish that were different.

SEVENTEEN | BRODY

It's close to 9 p.m. when I reach Carter's Villa and find everyone gathered in his study. He loves this kind of empowering shit.

"I need a word with you two first," Carter points at me and Nina and heads for his office.

Well, we both know what this is about. "What the hell did you two do?" He shouts right after I close the door behind me and follow close behind Nina.

"I'm not sure I know what you're talking about," she says, and I let her take the lead on this one.

"Don't play dumb with me, Reeves, I know you met with Richard last night, and then he disappeared off the face of the earth. So, I'm going to ask again, what the hell did you two do?"

"She stayed with me, not with Richard. He asked her to go up to his room, but she didn't." I defend her because in the end, it's both our mess.

"Relax, Stark, nothing will happen. Let's focus on how to steal the damn thing because so far I know I'm a prop," she ads with

"Don't you dare talk to me about focus, Reeves. You fucked up and it makes me want to skin you alive. I've been working on this for 2 years and you manage to fuck it up in 24 hours."

"For fucks sake, we did what we thought was right. We wanted to be one step ahead and it didn't go as planned but it's been taken care of, so back off."

"You know what, go. I can't do this tonight. You're all dismissed!"

"Dismiss me one more time like a dog, Carter, and I'll feed you your own tongue," she replies with a snarl and strolls out of the room.

"I think you're losing it, man," I say with a sigh, and I stare him in the eyes. I've known him for a long time to know that getting older scares him and he wants this job to be perfect.

"And I think you've been pussy whipped. Don't mess this up, Mason, or your father's men won't be your only problem."

Does he know about that? I don't like it one bit. "What are you talking about?"

"Don't play dumb with me, Brody. I know why you accepted this job before I even told you anything about it. Listen, we've been friends for a long time, Brody, so I'll let you in on a secret, but you have to promise me that you feel nothing for her," he asks with a clenched jaw and I have to swallow the lump in my throat before I answer.

Maybe I should think longer about it, but the truth is, there's nothing to think about. I can't feel anything for anyone. Not since they killed my heart and buried it 5 feet underground.

"I don't feel anything for her, Carter. It's just

physical attraction," I assure him and lie back in my chair, bracing myself for the secret he has to share, because somehow, I know that Nina is involved to some extent.

"Good, because Nina has feelings for you, and that has made her sloppy. She's our scapegoat, and she knows that there's always a scapegoat," he tells me and even though a wave of shock rolls through me, I keep my face expressionless and nod in understanding.

"I am here with one goal, and one goal only, to disappear, and for that I need the cash. My brother can never find me."

My entire life I have made mistakes that now cost me everything, and not killing my brother when I killed my father was one of them.

"You know what I don't understand, Brody. If you loved her so much, why didn't you join her?" he asks so easily and my eyes snap to his. I clench my teeth so hard that I hear a snap at some point, but I will not release the pressure.

I thought long and hard about what I should answer. If I should lie or tell him the truth, and the thing is, Carter is the only ally I have right, so I might as well keep him close. "She made me promise her I wouldn't. She made me promise that I'd live, but she didn't realize I wouldn't be able to live long without my heart."

Carter looks at me with pity in his eyes, along with something I can't decipher in his brown gaze. He probably will never understand the kind of love me and Eva had for one another and what it means to lose that.

"I don't understand it, but I definitely appreciate a promise. I trust you like I trust no one, brother," he shoots his bullet and I stand here, jaw ticking. I nod, unable to speak, and exit the office before he can say anything else.

For some reason, calling me that took me back to when Damien said similar words, just before I shot our father and the feeling I get deep in my chest frightens me.

I find Nina and Christina lounging in the living room, deep in conversation and when the brunette locks eyes with me, she smiles like what I would imagine a cat to smile like. "I want to go clubbing tonight, you guys up for it?"

I frown at the idea. I'm not much of a dancer but could use some drinking and relaxing.

"That sounds great," I hear Carter's voice behind me, and I turn around with a raised brow. Wasn't he all thunder a few minutes ago?

"You want to go clubbing? Are you okay?" Nina asks him and her eyebrows pinched together in confusion and curiosity.

Carter loves a good party at his Villa, but he's not much of a clubgoer, especially now that he's in his early forties. "I'm not great and would like to release some stress with alcohol and crappy music," he replies with a mischievous grin and after he sidesteps me, he extends a hand to a wide-eyed Christina.

Nina jumps to her feet and when it's clear that Christina and Carter will drive together, we decide to take a different car and we take mine, so I get behind the wheel and Nina climbs on the passenger seat.

"I never apologized to this beauty for ruining its paint," she says from my right, and I frown before I start it and drive off, close behind Carter.

"This beauty? How about me and the trauma you put me through?" I reply with a daring grin, and she bursts out laughing, quickly making me join her.

After a while, she wipes the tears from her eyes from all the laughing and throws me a one-sided smile. The ones I usually dazzle women with. "If you keep looking at me like that, *I* might provoke an accident this time," I whisper and swallow the lump in my throat and adjust my jeans which don't help my growing situation.

She turns her head away to avoid my fugitive gaze and I find myself reaching for her hand to kiss it. "I'm sorry, I didn't mean to upset you."

She doesn't say anything else to me and we continue to drive in silence for the remaining time, but I become grateful when I see Carter parking in the back of Blue Diamond Club. I park just behind him, and we exit the car in silence. Problem is that this club is usually packed, and I don't think we'll be lucky tonight.

"Did you guys see the queue though?" Nina says what I'm thinking as we start walking toward the club.

"I had someone add us to the VIP list and got us a table, don't worry," he smiles at her and grabs Christina's hand once more to lead her away.

When we reach the front of the queue, Carter speaks to the bouncer, and he quickly lets us inside. As soon as we step into the crowded room the loud music hits us like a drug rush and Nina is the first to start swaying her beautiful thick hips while we're being taken to our table. I stayed a few steps on purpose just to watch her body enjoy the flow of the music.

When we reach our table in a private corner of the club and I make myself comfortable on the sofa while Carter orders us a few bottles, a song I find it strange that I recognize starts playing, and Nina proceeds to move her hips on the rhythms of Renegade by Aaryan Shah and I feel compelled to watch her. Although her body is moving seductively and I can barely take my eyes off it, her gaze is what keeps my body temperature raised.

The glances she throws my way each time she opens her eyes after she's had them closed before the beat dropped, make me sink in my seat further and throw my head back. She plays with her hair, touches her body, and moves like she owns the damn song and it's the most beautiful thing I've ever seen.

I find it painful when my mind flies to Eva and remember how she's never been the wild type, but I loved her fiercely anyway, but Nina... she's a different breed.

A few long seconds later, Christina passes me what seems to be a PCP pill and I take both in my mouth without swallowing them because when one of the best songs known to clubs' history and sex playlists starts blasting in the speakers, I feel drawn to the brunette girl like a magnet. The weekend and Lily-Rose Depp, Fill the Void brings out the erotic side in any person and I almost want to tear her clothes right here and now when my hands connect to those damn curves of hers. She has her back to me when I embrace her from behind but doesn't hesitate to lean her head back on my chest and lose herself in the moment. A second later I turn her around and pull her mouth to mine in a slow kiss while I pass her the pill I've been saving for her.

She swallows it with a cheeky smile and starts kissing my neck, driving me insane with the slow burn.

EIGHTEEN | NINA

Whatever he gave me, is playing with my senses like nothing before. I've tried a few drugs in my ugly times era but nothing too strong because I had a sister to return to.

The moment Fill the Void started blasting from the speakers, a crazy idea shot through my head and now completely high on the pill and on the sensations, Brody brought up in me, I grab his hand and make a run for it while he follows me. I quickly find an empty private room with a sofa on it, and we enter it and close the door behind us.

I used to go to these types of clubs before and I know what these rooms are for and how to work with one, so as soon as we enter, I find the remote replay the song and turn the volume up, just enough to intoxicate me.

I instruct Brody to sit on the sofa and although he raises a brow in confusion, he does as I ask. I let the song lyrics guide my body like magic and I put every ounce of seduction that I'm capable of in the movements while my gaze never leaves Brody's.

I start walking slowly toward him while my body draws circles when he suddenly licks his lower lip in a lustful movement I smile and lick my own and I'm sure he moans and swears under his breath.

When I reach him, I climb onto his lap, and he quickly grabs my hips. I'm wearing a tight skirt like I normally do, and when I sit on top of him, it lifts up to my hips, leaving me almost bare in his lap. When his gaze roams down my body I rotate my hips skilfully and bite my lower lip when I feel the growing bulge from his pants.

He doesn't do anything inappropriate and treats this like a proper lap dance still, so I take his hand, place it on my throat, and dip down backward like I'd do a backflip, only to then be brought back up. The intensity of his stare sends electricity waves up my spine and the way his hand tightens its grip on my throat makes me shiver with pleasure. "I need to be inside you, now!" He growls with a ticking jaw and my pulse skyrockets. He lifts me with one hand while he unbuttons his jeans with the other.

He lifts his body off the sofa enough to push the jeans down. When I take his cock in my hand and guide him toward my entrance, he swears again. I let it slide in and the way he fills me up all the way to its root makes me clench around it and moan in pleasure.

"You're so wet for me. Always so wet for me, baby," he whispers on my lips just before he claims them, and I start bouncing on his dick. He grabs me by the throat again and with one hand on my hips he helps me up and down while he thrusts his dick so deep that I whimper each time. We've never tried this position before and the pain and pleasure that come from it makes me feel like I'm on cloud nine.

The sex or the pill.

The two greatest drugs in the world.

Separately they make you high, but together, they make you lose your fucking mind.

"Oh, God," I moan, my release creeping in.

"Yes, that's right. I'm your God, baby. Take me deep, milk my damn cock like a good girl," he growls and pushes his cum deep inside my belly, making me lose control. The orgasm takes over my body and I convulse all around his cock with loud moans. I fall on his chest all spent from the orgasm and effort and he hugs my body tightly against his.

"I love this," he whispers and for a minute my heart stops before I process what he actually said.

He meant the sex, not me.

I give him a weak smile and a nod while I jump off his lap and pull my skirt down.

"You're disappointed."

"No. Not disappointed. I just didn't expect that word from you."

He turns to look me in the eyes, now all tucked away and serious.

"Look, Nina. I like you," he says and takes my hands in his, making me question if he's the same man who usually has a gun at the back of his jeans. "I really do. You're beautiful, sexy and smart. You're everything a man could want, and the attraction is obvious between us. We just click, baby, and I want nothing more than to see you happy, but can you honestly tell me that after this is over, you'll leave everything and everyone to go hide with me on a deserted island? Can you honestly tell me that you'll choose me above everyone else?"

"I wish I could, but I have a sister who needs me, Brody."

He nods in understanding. "Maybe in another lifetime, Reeves."

"Maybe in another lifetime," I repeat the words and leave the room.

How did we get from we're not good for each other, to actually feeling bad that we can never be together so fast?

***

We've all gone through the plan 10 times in the last 3 hours, making sure that everything goes without a hitch. We have half an hour before we need to take off to the event, and we're all ready and waiting for the time to come.

I feel a bit of excitement deep in my belly and something tells me I missed this, even though I don't like it.

If everything goes according to the plan, we'll

get the fake necklace through the catering team and then Christina will wear it around her neck underneath her turtleneck dress. When it's finally time to wear the real piece, she'll come give me a hug and we'll swap necklaces as fast as we can without being noticed while Brody draws attention from me.

It looks like an easy plan, but the feeling of unease hasn't left me since last night.

"After you've swapped necklaces, Christina will go to the back of the kitchen, where Levi made sure all the security is out. Nina will return the fake to their team and disappear before they start asking questions. The replica is good, but we can never rely on it for too long, so as soon as you're all out, we'll meet on the helipad here where a chopper will be ready to take you away and bring you to Denver," he explains and shows us a building on the map, 2 blocks away from the event.

"What if they realize that it's a fake I'm giving back?"

"They have insurance covering the thing. If they can prove that's been stolen and it's not a scam, they'll most probably make more money than we will, so I have a feeling they won't care too much about it," he replies with a shrug before adding, "I need you to stay in pairs and have each other's backs in case shit goes down," Carter adds and my eyes quickly find Brody's who seems to have the same thoughts as me. We'll always have each other's back.

That's a silent promise.

"Simon and Jax will cover the camera feed to keep you covered at all times and I'll be on the coms as well to help you if you need me."

We all nod in understanding and Christina pulls me aside to speak to me privately. "Nina, I know we haven't been friends for that long, but I have a favor to ask. Please make sure money gets to my daughter if something happens to me. I beg of you, Nina," she begs me with sparkly eyes. We both know nothing will happen because we are good at what we do, and after all, the worst that could happen is getting caught by the police.

"I promise, Christina, but nothing will happen to you," I assure her and wrap my arms around her for a tight embrace, which she accepts with a deep sigh.

NINETEEN | NINA

We use taxis to get to the event because none of us have cars anymore. I sold mine a few hours back, Brody and Carter hid theirs in some kind of place until they can either sell them later or pick them up.

When we enter the hotel, Brody on my arm and Levi on Christina's, we analyze every corner of the place. We've done that before but now we just have to make sure that everything is still the same.

"Are you nervous?" Brody whispers in my ear while his grip is tight on my right hip making me hate the safe feeling that washes over me when he touches me.

"No. This ain't my first rodeo. You?"

"No. This ain't the most dangerous scene I've been in," he replies with a shrug.

With a nod and a wink, Christina and Levi disappear for their parts and I continue toward the line-up of girls. I suddenly realize that they arranged for the interview to be held in a room with a lot of security outside the door. "We have a problem," I say into my com and Brody nods and continues to explain the situation.

"We have 6 security guards at the door where the interview is held. I'm not sure how this will work, how we'll get the necklace out," he whispers in his com and smiles at me to cover our conversations from the others.

"Maybe we don't get the necklace, but maybe we get Christina inside instead. I'll need you to act surprized, Nina, so I'll speak to her privately," Carter says and shuts the com. I turn to Brody and look at him expectantly but he just shrugs.

"Let's get in line, stick to the plan, and hope that this will work, or all goes to shit."

I know he's right, but I do hope it won't go to shit. My sister's life depends on these 2 jobs. I get in line with Brody still at my hip and when I raise my eyes to his face, I find him looking at me with a smile. "What?"

"Nothing, you're shining for some reason."

"It's the makeup," I reply and feel the heat creep up my cheeks. What's wrong with me? I never blush.

Brody chuckles and soon we realize we're next in line. "Diana Munteanu," I say in a Romanian accent and the girl lets me inside the room. Brody has to wait outside for obvious security reasons and when I reach inside the room, I find a huge camera, 2 men and 3 women.

"Miss Munteanu, we're ready for you," one of the women says and brings up the shiny necklace. Wow, it truly is a beautiful thing.

She wraps it around my neck and locks it behind me, then gestures for me to sit on the chair in front of the camera. Although I am nervous now that I don't know Carter's plan or if any of it is going to work or not, I am keeping my cool calm while I sit down. "So, Miss Munteanu, how does it feel to be a part of Miss World?" the woman interviewing me asks with a tight smile.

I don't get to respond because the door opens on my left and Christina charges in like a storm and throws her arms around me while with one hand she dabs at my necklace, and I dab at hers to make sure the magnet system does its job and switches the two necklaces. She is quickly pulled away by the two men in the room and thrown out of the room, but she manages to speak before they close the door in her face. "I'm so sorry Diana, Sarah is gone. Sarah is dead," she shouts with tears in her eyes making it all seem so real that I get the urge to cry. For me, it's all too real because I know Sarah is her daughter's name, and that's how she managed to be so real.

"Who is Sarah, Miss Munteanu," the woman asks unfazed by Christina's interruption while tears stream down my cheeks.

"My daughter," I reply and get up to leave. I take the necklace off my neck and place it in the woman's hand before running out of the room. I find Brody waiting for me and when my hand touches him in urgency, a wave of relief washes over me.

We hurry toward the kitchen where we quickly find Levi and Christina. "Did it work?" I breathe out the words and when Christina's smile confirms it, I let out a breath of relief. "We have to go," Brody urges us and we all continue our hurried walk toward the back exit door.

When the cold air hits my face, I take a deep breath and we all walk toward the building our helicopter waits for us. The event is still quiet hell hasn't broken over and they're all still clueless, so I smile. "We did it."

"Don't jinx it, woman," Brody laughs and throws me onto his shoulder like a sack of potatoes, making me laugh and giggle like a schoolgirl.

I suddenly catch a glimpse of Levi's scowl but don't get a chance to question him because Brody starts running with me on his shoulder. "You're crazy."

"I'm crazy about you," he whispers and bites my ass cheek playfully making me scream. When we reach the building Brody lets me down on my feet and all 4 of us jump in the elevator. We ride it for a few minutes before we make it to the rooftop, where as promised, Carter waits for us with a helicopter and champagne. "You got it?"

"We got it," replies Christina, who shows him the piece and we all start cheering and whistle like it's a football game.

This feels so good, better than any other drug I've tried.

TWENTY | NINA

We arrived at the cabin in Glenwood Springs, Colorado a few hours after we managed to swipe the necklace and are now partying our asses off. We fucking deserve it. We've completed step one and are closer to our freedom than ever.

While Christina dances her ass off before flying back to Romania tomorrow morning, I take out my phone and shoot a message to Jessica, letting her know I'm okay and that I'll visit her soon.

"You should have something to drink," Brody brings me out of my thoughts talking in my ear to make sure I hear him over the loud music and hands me a beer. "I don't even know if you like beer."

"Beer's great," I reply and take the Budweiser he holds out for me. I take a big swig out of the bottle and smile at the way it goes down my throat.

"I'm gonna go to the bathroom," I say and get up from the sofa. I jump up the stairs as fast as I can because I can feel Brody's lingering gaze on my back. When I reach the bathroom door, it quickly opens and Levi stumbles out of it.

"Nina, the person I needed to see," he shouts. "Can I talk to you somewhere quieter?" he asks and although I'm confused by his request, I agree with a heavy sigh.

"Sure," I say and start walking toward the loft which I assume will be a bit quieter and we'll be able to understand each other. When we reach the loft, I turn around to face Levi, but he backhands me so quickly that I stagger back in shock and pain. The fucker has a good punch.

"You think you can give it to him under my nose but ignore me?" he shouts and throws me to the ground so fast that I don't have time to react or fight back.

I hit him in the face with my foot and manage to crawl away for a bit, but he manages to come back on top of me before I can get up and this time punches me in the face with full strength, almost stealing the breath from me. "Levi, you're drunk, let me go," I yell at him and struggle to throw him off me.

"You're not going anywhere until my dick is deep inside of you and you take it like the stupid whore you are."

He pushes down his pants to reveal a fully erect dick that I hope I get to cut off with my teeth if he's stupid enough.

I scream in frustration and wiggle hoping to get free. "I'll kill you with my bare hands if you don't let me go, Levi. I swear it on my mother's grave."

When he sees that I fight him too hard, Levi grabs the first thing he can get his hands on and hits me so hard that everything goes black for several seconds and I remain only faddily aware of what he does next, which is hike my dress up, snap my panties and forcibly push his dick inside me with a painful thrust. He only manages to push himself in a few times before I gain some of my consciousness back and realize that he stopped and I'm now empty, bare, and cold.

So fucking cold.

I fight the unconsciousness that wants to swallow me whole and when I get back to my senses, I first lay eyes on Brody's beautiful body and the way he throws punches at Levi's face. "I will fucking kill you for touching what's mine," he snarls, and I can almost hear the pain in his angry tone but I'm sure it's just his possessiveness. "But she deserves to do that after what you've done to her, you piece of shit," he adds in a growl and gets off Levi, enough to help me on my feet and hold me in his arms.

"I'm okay, Brody," I manage to whisper and suddenly feel the need to cover myself like Levi's seen already too much, Brody quickly understands so he takes off his denim jacket and puts it around my shoulders. I swallow the bitter taste in my mouth and take a few steps toward the bloodied man. "You wish he would've killed you when I'm done with you, Levi Jennings."

I turn my back on him, close my eyes, and take a deep steadying breath before addressing Brody. "Can you take him outside for me, please?"

"Of course, baby," he replies with an understanding nod and grabs the man from under his arms to carry him outside. Levi can hardly move his feet because the beating and the alcohol are probably making it hard for him, but Brody manages to slowly drag him down the stairs and I follow slowly behind them.

"I promised myself a long time ago that I'll break your arm off for fucking touching her," Brody snarls, and a second later Levi's scream pierces the silence of the woods with an echo.

When the rest of the partying crew spots us and the scene in front of them, they stop the music and follow us into the crisp air of Colorado.

"What happened?" Carter asks with a concerned look and is almost ready to jump at Brody's throat when I stop him.

"I need a knife," I say with a croaked voice addressing no one in particular but Jaxon is the one to hand me one without asking any questions. "You want to be inside of me, you piece of shit? How about I make sure you can never be inside anyone ever again," I grit out and while I know realization hits everyone by the sounds they all make, I grab Levi's pants, pull them down and look Brody in the eye, somehow expecting him to tell me this is wrong, but when he nods his head slightly, I look back at Levi and in one swift motion I cut his dick off making him scream in pain for just a second before Brody pushes a piece of cloth in his mouth to shut him up.

"Nina, did he touch you?" Christina comes close but doesn't dare to touch me.

"He did more than touch me," I whisper back, and she gasps in shock.

Adrenaline finally over, I double over on my palms and knees, and let out the most heart-clenching scream, reliving the trauma of being raped when I was 15. Someone gets on their knees next to me and lets me lean on them while I sob uncontrollably.

They will not break me this time.

I won!

I got my revenge.

"What do you want us to do with him," Brody whispers in my ear and I don't have to think too hard about it, I take the gun from the back of his jeans and shoot Levi 2 times. I know I haven't hit anything vital. I want him to not die for hours because I want the motherfucker to suffer.

"I'm keeping this from now on, in case anyone else gets any more ideas," I snarl and look around to the remaining men. Brody helps me back on my feet and I return to the cabin to clean up and forget any of it happened.

I won't let the fucker play with my mind, because that means he wins, and we've established that he didn't.

I did.

"Come, I'll draw you a bath," Christina wraps

her arms around me and I shake it off. "Stop pitying me, I'm fine!"

"I know you're fine. You're the strongest woman I fucking know. I'm just cuddling my friend who had a rough day, that's all," she replies and ushers me upstairs like a pissed-off parent.

I manage a broken smile and do as I'm told. When I reach the bathroom, I lose the clothes I have on and succumb in the hot water.

TWENTY-ONE | BRODY

A few hours later I find Nina on the front steps of the cabin and sit down next to her. "He's gone."

"They just moved him deeper in the woods, no one will save the fucker this time. I promise you," I assure her, and she sighs deeply.

She doesn't look at me when she whispers, "Thank you."

I take her chin with two fingers and make her look at me when I ask my next question. "Are you okay?"

I can see her jaw clenching and swallowing hard before she manages to answer. "I am now. Thank you for being there when it mattered."

"I'll always be there," I find myself whispering back before I can stop. When it comes to this girl, I want to kill anyone that looks her way, and now this fucker... he touched her.

He touched what's mine and I feel like I'm losing my mind while I try not to go out there and torture the fuck out of him for a few long hours and then feed him to the wolves bit by bit, limb by limb.

Deep in thought, it takes me some time to realize that she's crying again. "Why would you say that? We both know it's a lie."

Words seem to fail me right now and I can't

seem to find the strength to contradict her. Nothing I'll say will change what's happened or the things I said to her in the past.

"Do I not deserve to be loved, Brody?" she asks a few minutes later and her question leaves me speechless once again and I'm afraid that no matter what I say won't be the right answer. "You deserve the world, baby."

She sniffles and jumps to her feet like she might run away, but it's only a second before she turns to face me. "Then love me, please. If you can ever love someone again, please, love me," she says in a cracked voice, and I feel my shell of a heart fucking break in my hollow chest, leaving me shocked, breathless, and dumbfounded.

"Nina, baby, you should never beg for any man's love, because they'll be fucking lucky to have your love," I say as soon as I jump on my feet.

"But I don't want any man. I want you, Brody. I want you, because I love you, so please, please..." She breaks down and pleads with tears in her eyes and when my heart starts to hurt in my chest, I understand. Seeing her like this makes me finally understand it all.

My heart is free and beating wild again.

For her.

My heart is breaking to see her like this, and I only felt like this once before, when I was utterly in love and realization hits me like a train and knocks the breath out of me.

It's like I've been blind all this time when it's always been her.

All the things I said I couldn't do for her since the beginning, that's exactly what I've been doing. I've been protecting her, making love to her, and cherished her. It only takes me two steps before I'm in front of her and I grab her face with both my palms to make sure what I'm about to say will be heard and understood. "Oh, baby... my foolish girl, I have been in love with you since the moment I saw you that day downtown. I have been in love with you from the first kiss, the first smile, and the first snarl, baby. I am so fucking in love with you that it hurts. It physically hurts me, Nina, because this damn thing has been dead for too long and now it's almost unbearable to see you like this," I say and point at my heavy raising chest. "I love you, baby. I have been a fool to think that wasn't love because honestly, I forgot how it felt but I fucking love you and there's no denying that anymore."

I brush my lips softly against hers and when she whimpers, I can't contain myself anymore and give her everything I have through this one kiss. There's no tongue, no ass-grabbing, just plain passion. I have to ignore all the things I want to do to her now that she's mine because she's been through a lot tonight. "I love you, do you hear me?" I whisper on her soft lips once again and she sniffles with a laugh. "Now let's get you inside, you're freezing."

"I want you to fuck me," she whispers back on mine, taking me by surprise.

"Are you sure?" I ask in a daze. I don't think that's the best idea, but if that's what she needs, I'll give her anything.

She takes a deep breath and starts undoing my jeans button. "I need you to erase the memory. Erase him, please. His touch, his feel, I need to not remember that anymore," she reasons with me and now her request makes sense.

I take her face in my palms again and kiss her lips softly before taking her in my arms and carrying her upstairs to my room.

When we get there, I lay her on the bed and don't leave her gaze while I take my clothes off. First my jeans, then my T-shirt, and only my boxers remain on.

She watches me with desire written all over her face.

"You tell me when it's too much."

"It'll never be too much," she replies and removes her dress. Her words set me on fire completely and I remove her panties slowly. She gasps when I touch the inside of her thigh and then my fingers reach toward her wetness.

I fucking love how wet she gets for me, and I could get off on this alone. I kiss the inside of the thigh I just touched and the woman on my bed arches her back and grabs my hair.

I push my boxers down my thighs and after I claim her lips with raw passion, I enter her folds in one slow thrust. Tonight, I want to take my time with her sweet pussy because I'm very aware it could be the last time I feel her.

"You take me so good, baby," I whisper on her lips, my right hand on her hip and my left on the bed, and continue with slow ins and outs while she pushes her hips to meet my thrusts even deeper.

"Harder, Brody," she pleads, and I do as she asks and pick up my speed with a groan. A second later I decide to switch it up and with a swift move, I flip her on her belly and enter her again before she has time to protest.

"If you want harder, I'll give it to you harder," I say between heavy breaths and continue to slam into her ass like a teenage boy. I'll also feel like a teenage boy when I'm going to come from the view her ass gives me when it wiggles with each slam.

"I'm coming, Brody," she wheezes at that exact moment I reach for her clit with my right hand, driving her over the edge. She tries to stifle her ecstasy screams by biting into the pillow when I follow her with my own sweet release.

"This is exactly what I needed. Thank you," she says a minute later once we've both caught our breaths.

"I've never been thanked for sex before," I joke.

"Well, you should have been because you're doing a great job at it," she replies and kisses my lips.

There's no way she's spending another minute away from my sight, but at the same time, I have to have an urgent conversation with Carter and the fact that her stomach is growling, gives me a great advantage.

"I'm gonna go bring you something to eat, okay?"

She nods softly and cuddles up in my sheets, so I put my clothes back on and run to Carter's bedroom before getting her the promised food. "Carter, you in here?"

"I'm kind of busy, go away Mason," he shouts from behind the door, and I roll my eyes before barging in. Was I expecting to find Christina riding him like a cowgirl? Nope. Do I care? Also, nope. "I can see that, but it's kind of urgent, so Christina can finish herself off," I add with a knowing grin and the redhead flips me the bird as a result of my intrusion.

"Fuck you, Brody," she throws at me while she jumps off Carter and picks up her clothes from all over the floor.

"What's so urgent that it couldn't wait, Brody?" Carter asks me with a deep frown on his face, all while he just makes himself comfortable under his sheets. This is beyond disgusting.

"The deal we had is off. Nina can't be the scapegoat anymore," I explain all while I'm trying to avoid looking below the neck area. Seeing Carter's dick is the last thing I need right now.

I think it's safe to say the fucker shocks me when he laughs. He fucking laughs in my face. "The plan is set in stone, Masoni! I can't save your girlfriend this last minute, especially after she killed Levi."

"Don't be an asshole, he deserved it. Make Christina the scapegoat for all I care, or one of the twins, but leave her out of it or I'll tell her everything right now!" I shout at him hoping to make my message clear.

I turn around to exit the room when I hear him jumping off the bed and I turn around in time to see a punch coming at my face. "What the actual fuck?"

"I fucking told you not to catch feelings for her! You swore it wouldn't happen, but here we are," he shouts back while I fix my hurting jaw. The fucker knows how to throw a good punch. He always has.

"Well, you're the one who kept saying she's necessary for this job and how you've known her for years. How can you throw her under the bus like that?"

"That was her purpose, Mason. What's so hard to understand? She's always been linked with the Phantoms, so she can easily pass as the head."

"You brilliant fucker! They'll come for her for the necklace anyway, isn't it?"

"Now you get it. Look, if it's worth anything, I'll make someone else the scapegoat, but that doesn't mean she's safe. I can't change what's been done already."

"Don't you worry about my girlfriend, Carter. I'll protect her after the job, just keep your end so I won't have to end you," I throw at him before I exit his room and stroll toward the kitchen.

Fuck.

Everything is so fucked up.

I'm going to kill this motherfucker after we finish.

I'm making my way toward the kitchen when a set of headlights grab my attention from the outside. "What the fuck?"

That's all I get to utter before I see the projectile hit the first floor and the blast sends me crashing toward the wall behind me. My ears start ringing while smoke and dust fill my lungs and make me cough violently. My thoughts are all jumbled up, but one name stands out in the chaos.

Nina.

I need to get to Nina.

I force myself onto my feet while pain shoots up from my ribs to my upper back, but I ignore it and start running towards the stairs, or what's left of them. I don't get to take a few steps when Carter grabs my arm and drags me back. "They're gone, you can't save them. Let her go, Mason!"

I fucked up too many times in this lifetime and she doesn't deserve to be another collateral. I won't allow it.

Not after what they did to Eva.

TWENTY-TWO | NINA

"Christina?" I shout between coughs, trying to pinpoint my friend's location. I know she should be in the room in front of mine but all that's left of that room is dust and debris, with no sign of the red head. "Brody? Carter?" I try again as hell unleashes downstairs and voices fill the ringing in my head.

I finally think to get my phone's flashlight out and when I do, I find Christina at my left, bruised and bloody under a huge piece of concrete. Her vacant eyes tell me that she is not with us anymore and all I can do is double over and stifle a cry.

"Brody?" I shout again and start running downstairs when his commanding voice sounds in the ruin.

"Stay there, Reeves. Don't come down here!" He uses a cold tone, making me wince.

"Hello, big brother," I hear a foreign voice and something in his accented timbre makes me swallow hardly. He has a brother?

I hear shuffling and guns clicking and I know that if I descent these steps, or what's left of them, I am as good as dead, so I clench my jaw and wait, completely rooted in the spot.

"I will not fight you, if we leave now and let the rest of them leave," Brody says and my heart clenches. What's going on? Why would his brother do this to him? "Do we have a deal?"

"Brody, no! Don't do this!" I say when I realize what he's suggesting and start down the stairs once again when his pleading voice breaks my heart and makes me kneel.

"Nina, please. Don't you dare come down here," he says, and I have to bite the inside of my cheek hard if I want to stay put. I need to find the others because I need those cars. Jess needs me to see this through... She needs me more than him.

"Oh, you're on a first-name basis. How cute," he mocks his brother.

"Do we have a deal, Damiano?"

His brother chuckles, "I do not care about these rats, brother. I only want you," his brother replies in a beautiful English and a deep tone that gives me goosebumps all over my body and after some more shuffling and muffled noises, I see the car headlights disappear from my sight and realize that he's gone.

What the fuck just happened?

The first thing that I do is get up, let him deal with whatever family issue he has and find the rest of the crew, if they made it out alive. Still being on the first floor, I start searching the rooms that are still intact from the explosion when a voice calls my name from outside. "Nina? You alive?"

When I look out the window, I find Carter holding two bags. Of course he ran at the first sight of trouble. He wouldn't be Carter if he didn't betray us when he first got the chance.

I descend the steps and punch him in the face first before I listen to his bullshit. "You bastard!" I grit out and clench my teeth, trying hardly not to punch him again.

"What was that for?" he asks with anger.

"You ran and let us all to die," I shout at him and shove at his chest.

"I had a split second. I was downstairs and I decided to run and I'm not going to apologise for it. If you are as smart as you say you are, you know you would've done the same. Now, are you done?" he replies and grabs both my hands to stop me from getting at him again.

"You were always a piece of shit. I'm done with you. I'm going after him," I say with a sigh and turn on my heel when he grabs my elbow and spins me around to face him once more.

"Wow wow, hold on, that's a suicide mission," he says and keeps his grip on my elbow, as if I'm going to run away from him. I do think about it long and hard, but I'm also smart enough to know that I don't have a chance without him and the others. I'm not an assassin. I'm merely a thief who's skilled with a gun, but these guys... the mafia is not something I ever dreamed of facing.

But here I am.

"So, you're just going to leave him there?" I ask

in a pleading voice, hoping that he cares about his friend at least a tiny bit.

Truth be told, I know this job is done if we don't get Brody back, so I know he is just trying to leverage me.

Carter takes a long time to answer, so he takes his right hand through his hair and sighs deeply before doing so, "Listen, sweetie. You don't know them like I do. You do not mess with the Masoni. You don't mess with the Mafia in general, but with them? We don't fucking stand a chance."

"You think I don't know that? I don't want to face the Mafia, Carter, but we need him or this job is finished before it even started, and I'm counting on it. My sister is counting on it. She's counting on me. You faced them before, you helped him hide," I plead my case and I can see in his body's possition change that I'm almost through to him.

If something's going to convince Carter to help me, is the fact that he'll lose the cars if we don't get Brody back. "That's exactly why I ran, because I'm a dead man if they catch me, just like your boyfriend is."

"I'm not giving up on him. We can't do this without him, and you know it. We have a shot at this before they get out of state, which is a few hours. Are you with me or not?"

This conversation is over. Now it's up to him to make the last statement.

"The cars are passing through tomorrow

night. So, we have less than 48 hours to get him out and make sure his brother doesn't ruin our plans. Got it?"

"Trust me, I know...What about the JJs and Simon?" I ask referring to the twins and what's remained of our crew.

"Jax and Simon were fucking in the woods, so are without a scratch and Jason was smoking outside, so he's waiting on my signal." He explains and I smile sadly at the thought of Simon and Jax. They used to tease each other so much, I guess it makes sense.

"Tell me about his brother. Why would they want him dead?"

"It's not a pretty story. Are you sure about this?"

I nod and lean on a tree. God, we're lucky there's a full moon.

"Brody killed his father, the capo of the mafia. Now his brother is the Capo, and they need to avenge their old one. If you ask me, it was a justified kill, but even in Damiano's eyes... Brody is guilty and needs to receive the death penalty."

Obviously, Carter doesn't care about going into more detail and I know I'm going to have to be patient and get the rest of the story from Brody, so for now I accept the breadcrumbs I'm getting. "The death penalty... I read that somewhere. It's bad, isn't it?"

"It's an old tradition, where every member of the mafia can slice up a part of his body a day, keeping him alive and well for months before his wounds get infected and he dies."

"That's disgusting and barbaric," I say with a cringe.

"It is, but it's their law."

It might be their law, but I hope Brody doesn't have to go through this.

TWENTY-THREE | BRODY

"I never knew my own brother would hunt me down like I'm a damn dog!" I spit through gritted teeth. I knew this day would come, but I just hoped I had a bit more time before he caught up with me.

In my world, you never get away with what I did.

"You brought this upon yourself, Bruno! Don't try to make me pity you, because I won't. You knew the consequences for your acts, and you did it anyway!"

Do I deserve any of it? Probably. But I'm sure everyone being in my place would've done the same. Father was one of the worst Capo's to exist in the Masoni Mafia and everyone knew that, but I could never imagine that he'd go that far as to kill my wife, the woman of my life, and the future mother of his grandchildren.

But that was Vincenzo Masoni. A heartless son of a bitch.

"It's so easy for you to blame me when you've got everything you wanted from what I've done. Don't act like my actions didn't benefit you! And never call me that name again!" I rage at him and am happy to be shackled up, so I don't add him to my kill list.

"You're right. You lost the rights to that name the minute you killed our father and fled the country."

"Fuck you, Damiano! Fuck you! Just kill me already and be done with it."

Damiano laughs sheepishly and narrows his gaze on me. I don't know how two brothers can be so different looking. While I took after my mother with lighter brown hair and blue eyes, he took after our father with his light brown honey eyes and dark brown hair. "Oh no, brother. What I have planned for you is way better than death. Death is boring. What we have in store for you is so bad that you'll beg us to kill you."

"You're giving me the death penalty, isn't it?"

"Of course, brother. The other Capo's want to make an example out of you and I'm more than happy to oblige."

Of course he is.

If there's someone who acts like father, it's Damiano. He's always been a deranged son of a bitch and I know he's going to enjoy every minute of this.

I just hope and pray to God that Nina won't do anything stupid.

"Can I tell you a secret? I never loved Eva. I used her to get to you and eventually to Father. It worked like a charm in the end," he confesses, and I feel the world crashing around me. "I knew that if Father felt like he was losing you or worse, both of us because of some pussy, he'd do something irrational."

"So she died because you manipulated all of us. They both did?" I breathe the words. "Our baby died because of you?" I whisper more as a statement rather than a question before I jump onto my feet and while trying to balance myself in the moving car, I throw both hands at him in an attempt to punch him but it's not much I can do before two of his men throw me back on the bench. "I will kill you, even if it's the last thing that I do, brother."

He smiles arrogantly and opens his mouth to speak but he doesn't get to because suddenly I'm not on the bench anymore but on the roof of the van as we spin in the air. Something's hit us from the side.

Or rather said, someone.

TWENTY-FOUR | NINA

I open the back door of the white van and find Brody right next to it, so I grab him by under his shoulders and help him out. "Hi, handsome," I whisper and kiss his bruised cheek.

"You're crazy!" he utters.

I chuckle. "I thought we already established that silly. C'mon, we gotta go."

"What should we do about your brother?" Carter is the one to bring up when I place Brody onto the passenger seat of my car.

He thinks about it for a second. "Blow them up."

"Mason, that's two Capo's deaths on your hands. Are you sure?"

"Blow the son of a bitch up," he spits blood and swallows with a grunt.

Carter nods and I drive off towards our meeting point before we need to drive of toward the point where we have good vantage to grab the cars. Behind me, it the rear-view mirror I see the van going up in flames as if made of plastic.

"It's time you told me the truth, Brody Mason."

He doesn't hesitate before answering all the unasked questions and that almost makes me smile. "My name is Bruno Masoni and I am... I was heir to the Masoni mafia of Milano."

"Brody Mason. It makes sense, and I did hear you speak in flawless Italian before, but you have to give me more. Why is your brother out to get you? Don't you have a code or something?"

I don't know much about Mafia but from my limited knowledge I know their whole lives are or should be led by a code.

"We do, and I broke it when I killed the Capo, our father," he explains further and although it feels like he's feeding me breadcrumbs, it's only because I can't put it all together.

He killed his own father...

"That's fucked up, Brody," I reply with a frown.

"Not as fucked up as him murdering my wife while forcing me to watch. It's a long and painful story, Nina, and it all started because my brother fell in love with my wife. My father despised the thought of us both being at each other's throats because of a woman, so he killed her and in a fit of rage, blinded by pain, I killed him. Simple as that. Since then, my brother vowed to bring justice to the Masoni Clan to revenge their capo, while also enjoying it because he blames me for Eva's death rather than our father."

"Where do I fit in this story?" I ask.

"If my brother realizes the amount of power you have over me... how much I love you, then history will be repeating itself and I cannot allow that, baby. I have to keep you safe even if it means going our separate ways."

I wish it were that simple.

"That's not an option, Mason. My sister needs this job to end well. She's sick and needs a lot of money for treatment," I explain briefly without going into too much detail. It's neither the time nor the place.

"You shouldn't have come for me," he whispers and avoids eye contact.

I sigh and take a deep breath when I actually want to smack him in the face. "Are you even listening to me, Brody? That wasn't a fucking option!"

"It was the only option. What you did was stupid and reckless, Reeves," he counters, and I have the sudden urge to punch him, so I stop the car and jump out to take a deep breath.

He follows suit in an instant, so I face him with anger and shove at his chest with each question. "Oh, we're back to Reeves now? What's next? You're going to say that what you said last night was a mistake? You got carried away?"

"That's not what's happening, but Reeves this is not how it was supposed to go, and you know it. What we feel for each other puts everything at risk," he pleads and stares deep into my eyes as if he's trying to read something I'm not saying in them.

"And these thoughts just came back to you? What about last night when you were deep inside me, and you were telling me how much you loved me?"

"I'm not saying that I don't love you, love, just that I don't think that we're supposed to be together. Maybe we're just not meant to be," he replies with a hard face, leaving me speechless.

This can't be the same man that made love to me last night.

"Wow, you're a real piece, you know that, Mason? You're right, I should've let your brother do whatever horrors he had planned for you," I say with hatred. "If I'm such an incommodity for you, you can drive the damn car yourself! I'm done here!"

I start walking toward Carter's car with tears in my eyes, while Brody calls my name a couple of times, but I ignore him and jump in the back next to Simon and they drive off without a word.

I am so done begging for his love.

TWENTY-FIVE | NINA

The time has finally come to finish this once and for all and then to part our ways. I'm driving with Carter, Simon's with Brody and the twins have their own car. The plan was a lot different a couple of days ago, when we had 2 extra people, but now we have to manage with just the six of us. Carter, Brody and Jax will be the ones to highjack the train and grab the cars while we help them by driving perfectly in sync with the train.

The first thing I do before all this goes down, I take my phone out of my pocket and shoot Jess a quick message. *'It's happening. See you soon, Monkeyface.'*

"When we take the cars and are ready to drive off, I need you to go south with Jason and Simon, while the three of us spread out north." He explains and I nod.

"Okay."

"Everyone in position?" he asks in the coms, and everyone answers briefly.

It's 10:05 pm and it's just gotten dark, so everything is more difficult, but we've practiced driving in line with the train in our 4x4 cars through the woods. The three men just have to get inside the train unnoticed and try to stop it if possible, and if that's not possible, then the cars might suffer a bit.

"Nina, I'm sorry."

"We're not doing this right now Brody. Drop it," I say through gritted teeth just as the speeding train approaches, its rhythmic clatter echoing through the Aspen mountains.

"It's show time," Carter announces and proceeds to open the window all the way down. He grabs the crossbow from the back seat and throws a line on his section of the train. They have to make it underneath to the openings.

We could just blow some shit up and make it noisier and faster, but that might attract too much unwanted attention, so we decided on doing this as quietly and as swiftly as possible.

With cars this precious, we're absolutely certain that they have security with them, so my part now is to make sure I can help make their job easier, so I stop my car and quickly jump on with Simon. He takes me closer to the last car of the train and I jump onto the ladder. This thing is moving really fast, but we are faster.

The problem is that this train has 10 compartments when we only knew about 6 and the cars were supposed to be in C1, C3, and C6. This just makes it harder but not impossible, it just means that to disable the security and open the doors I have to go in from underneath, so that's what I do.

These trains were built for this, so they always have extra hidden exit doors in case things go south, like right now, so what I'm doing is opening the small hatch door from C10 while trying to not drop onto the tracks and meet my maker sooner than I'd planned.

When I've managed to open the hatch as slowly and as silently as possible, I throw in a gas grenade that should take all of them out before I climb in there, but if it won't, then I'll have to fight my way through. I wait a few minutes for the grenade to make its victims, put my mask on, and then go in. I quickly look around me and ready my silent gun but am relieved to see that the grenade made my job easier.

"C10 is empty, moving onto C9," I share with the others, knowing that Brody is coming in from C1.

"Fuck! C1 is also empty," we hear Brody's voice.

I move slowly through the empty compartments with my hand raised and when I reach the door, I open it very slowly. The problem is that these doors have no windows so I have no idea what awaits me on the other side, but when I step inside I find another empty one. "C9 is Empty. I think they're in C7, 6, and 5," I say, hand on the handle of the C8 door, and when I reach inside and it's empty, I move toward the other one quicker. "C8 is also empty. The next one should be it."

"C2 and C3 are also empty. You might be right,

Nina," Brody replies just as I open the door and inch and listen for any kind of movement from inside the C7. When nothing reaches my ears, I throw the door open and realize that it's not C7, so that means the car won't be in 5, it'll be 4. "Brody, wait! 7 is empty, so that means C4 has one car. Proceed carefully."

When I reach compartment 6, I open the door slowly and throw in a gas bomb. I wait exactly 30 seconds before I throw the door open, and a rain of bullets start flying my way.

The problem is that I can't just shoot without aim and damage the cars, or we'll never sell them, even on the black market, so I bide my time and wait for the smoke to clear. A minute later, when the compartment becomes clearer, I see a security guard and shoot him clean. I then spot 3 more and remain hidden behind two crates while bullets continue to pour.

"C6 is putting up a good fight," I breathe in my com and when I find a clear moment, I come out of hiding and shoot two of the guys. "I take that back," I add to my team with a snort, just as a bullet grazes my left arm and I wince in pain.

Motherfucker. I jinxed it.

"You didn't pick the right day to fuck with me, bitch!" shouts the last guy, and I smile to myself.

"So did you, buddy. So did you!" I shout back and come out to shoot again only to realize that I'm out of bullets and that he's already coming for me, leaving me no time to load my gun, so what I do is take good aim and throw it at his head, only to win me a second of lost attention so I can throw one of my knives too.

When my gun hits him good in the eye, he swears and staggers back, giving me enough time to throw two knives. One sticks in his right leg and the other one misses his left arm by a few millimeters but makes him drop the gun.

He cries in pain, but I don't give him enough time to grab his gun and I take off running and punch him with all my force. He tries to punch back but I manage to dodge it and push my foot in his stomach. I then roll on the floor, grab his gun, and shoot him once in the middle of his forehead.

"Sweethearts, my job here is done," I say in my coms as I push the button to open the side door from where the car will fly. Now Simon has to come in with the gear to open this baby up and drive off with it.

"So is C5," replies Carter when I jump back onto Simon's car and switch places with him.

Brody doesn't say anything, but I see him flying with the car onto the road. We've picked this spot to hijack the train because there's a forest road next to the tracks that helps us keep the cars as intact as possible, so the value doesn't go down.

"Let's get going guys, something up on the radio," we hear Jason announcing on the com, so that's what we do, we drive off in our directions, as we've been instructed by Carter but after a few minutes into the drive something doesn't sit well with me.

I look into my rear-view mirror only to find an empty road and no one behind me. "Guys? I think I've lost you," I whisper with a frown, unease filling my stomach and when my eyes return to the road ahead of me, my heart sinks.

"No..." I deny it even if I know what's happening.

I'm the scapegoat.

I'm the person the feds will be satisfied catching for now so that they can get away with the cars and sell them without fear of being caught.

"I'm so sorry, baby. He gave me his word that he won't do this, but he lied."

"And you chose to lie to me. You could have warned me," I say in a broken whisper. "Just always remember that I'm coming for you, Carter."

Before more pleading and apologies come through the com, I press the small button on the earpiece and with hazy eyes, I remove it from my ear. Now I focus only on the bright red and blue lights that are fast coming my way.

Yes, I could turn around and try to lose them, but that would only make my case worse. If I just stay put, I can spin a story of how he's kidnapped my sister and forced me to do this. I can get out of this if I play my cards right, so I slam the brakes and stop in the middle of the road.

When the cop cars stop a few meters from me, I get out of the car with hands behind my head to show that I'm cooperative, so I don't get shot. It's only a minute before one of the cops approaches me and cuffs my hands behind my back while also reading my rights.

The standard bullshit procedure.

But I let them. I let them smash my head against the car, I let them shove me in the back seat, and let them throw all the accusations they want because this is not the end, it's just the

fucking beginning.

TWENTY-SIX | NINA

I don't know how long it's been since I've been thrown in here when someone opens the door to my solitary room and light floods the shithole.

I wince in pain and cover my eyes because my pounding head can't take the strain on my eyes when he places a set of handcuffs around my already bruised wrists. "Rise and shine, baby, you've been summoned."

"You sound like this is a fantasy land," I croak and follow the shithead through a long well-lit corridor.

"Oh, it will be, baby girl," he smirks, making me cringe and wish I could bash his head in.

When he opens a room to his left and pushes me inside, I have the urge to run toward the mirror window and growl like a feral animal. I've been in jail before, but never in prison or one of these rooms.

After staring through the one-way mirror for a long minute, to make sure I show them that I'm not scared, I take a sit on the chair and wait for the shitshow to start. It doesn't take long before a man in a beautiful dark navy suit comes in with a cup of coffee in one hand and a folder in the other.

His green eyes search my face for any emotion and his chiselled face remains as expressionless as mine.

"Nina Reeves, my name is Sean Condreu. Coffee?" he asks casually and takes the sit on the opposite side of the table.

"I'm fine," I grit out. "What can I do for you detective?"

I know how this interrogation works. He asks me stupid questions, reads me between the lines, and takes notice of my behavior.

"Oh, so you are as smart as they write about you, Miss Reeves. What gives?"

"Other than your expensive ass suit? Your confidence, your analyzing eyes, and your sweet chatter. The first thing you did when you walked in here was look at my hands and I can bet you a thousand dollars that you hate that useless guard for not handcuffing me to the table. Would you fire him? Please fire him."

The man laughs and relaxes in his chair. "I can't fire him although I hoped to make that happen for some time now. He truly is useless and a piece of shit on top of that. As for the handcuffs, here," he says and brings out a key from his pocket. He unlocks my cuffs, takes them off, and places them in his pocket, making me narrow my eyes at him.

I can't say that this move didn't surprise me.

"I'll let you in on a secret, Miss Reeves. It takes me about 2 minutes to read a person and decide if I'm a good cop or a bad cop. With you, it took me less than a minute. You're not a bad guy, you're just a young girl who's been misled by others. Am I on the right path?"

I do something that I know cops hate, which is mimic his posture and smirk. "Look, Sean, I'm not some damsel in distress. If I'm here, it must mean that I did some stuff to get me in here."

"Oh, I know you're not," he says a beat later and his left hand goes into his pocket. When he brings it back out, I can't hide my shock even if I want to.

Son of a bitch.

Sean places the item next to his coffee cup and I close my eyes for a second. Carter never needed the money off the necklace, he just needed it to make sure I didn't get out very quickly, so he had the necklace with him all this time, until he somehow placed it in my car.

Is this what Brody meant when he said Carter promised I wouldn't be the scapegoat anymore?

Fuck!

"I can see you recognize it, so there's no need to lay all the details out for you. We know you and your crew stole this from L.A. about a week ago. I have to admit, it was a flawless job, but you didn't consider one tiny detail. When the team has to place the necklace back in its vault, they use some kind of sprays and chemicals to sanitize it and to make sure that if someone tries to break the vault and grab it, they'll be instantly poisoned. A bit dramatic if you ask me, but effective nonetheless because when they placed the necklace in its case, the fake melted away in a matter of seconds, so that's when they realise what you've done."

I raise an eyebrow waiting for more, but I'm met with complete silence for a very long minute. All I can do now is stare at the beautiful necklace that sits royally in Sean's big palm.

This is what I get for losing my head and one way or another, I fucking deserve it.

I never should've trusted any of them, but especially Brody Mason.

"And the cars? God, I must say, you are good, but I'm better. We found you at the scene and as soon as we stopped the train, guess what, the train was empty, and all the security was gassed off or shot. I can't charge you for stealing them, because we don't have any evidence, but we have enough evidence to charge you as an accomplice and for stealing the necklace. You curious how many years you could get for that? In my experience, the minimum is 10 with a bail of millions. So, tell me, *Nina*, do you know someone willing to pay a few million to get you out?"

He knows the answer to that question, and he knows that I don't want to spend a decade in prison.

I can't.

"Here's the deal, you can sign it right now. You give me the name or names of the leads and I can cut down a deal for 5 years right now," he explains and pushes the open folder in front of me.

I would gladly give them the names even without the deal, but a sentence cut in half or even more. I can live with that.

So, I grab the folder, read through it, check for the court seal because he wouldn't be able to offer a plea without it, and sign it. "Carter Stark and Brody Mason. Those are the names you want."

It's so funny how this guy thinks he's the smartest one in the room.

He's smart, but not the smartest.

They will never find them because they're probably in Alaska by now.

"Do you know where they were going to hide?"

"I might, but what's in it for me?"

The detective laughs and narrows his gaze at me. "I'll tell you what, Miss Reeves. You give their location, and I'll make sure they don't make your life a living hell, do we have a deal?"

"We had a few destinations in mind, Costa Rica, Panama, but if they're smart enough, you won't find them there. If I were still with them, I would've suggested Nunivak Island or a Country with a non-existing extradition treaty."

"Nunivak, isn't that in Alaska?" he asks with a frown.

"Good at Geography, paint me impressed," I put on my most charming smile.

One thing is clear. I need friends in this place,

or I will not survive it.

"I'm good at so many other things, Miss Reeves," he replies with a wink.

"Can I ask for a favor? I have one phone call, don't I? I need to call my sister," I whisper the last bit and swallow the lump that's lodged in my throat.

"I'll make sure you get that today. Expect a visit from a state lawyer and I'll also make sure you get placed in a normal cell."

"How nice of you, detective."

With that, he inclines his head, grabs the folder and the coffee, and leaves me in the room by myself for several minutes.

TWENTY-SEVEN | NINA

It's been over a week, even if it felt like a year and although I've been promised a lawyer, I don't know what for when I'm not supposed to go to trial anymore. Things have been quiet around here and I'm sure I have to thank that douche detective for it.

It's 3:30 pm which means shower time if you're up for it, so I grab my things and head straight for the warm water. Yes, warm, not hot. I'm surprised it's not ice-cold, so I'm not complaining. Food's been okay for a prison and the women around don't get too close. So far, they've kept their distance and I'm grateful for that.

After the detective left, someone brought in a phone and I tried calling Jessica, but she never picked up, so now I have no way of contacting her. I was hoping Sean, or my fucking lawyer would come around so I can at least get the clinic's number, but none of them showed up so far and I don't know if my sister is okay or not.

I jump in the shower and turn on the water. I close my eyes for a few seconds to enjoy the warm liquid running down my body when I feel a whoosh of air next to me, and then someone shouts, "Watch out!"

I open my eyes in an instant and jump back. I don't know why but I know it's the right decision. As soon as my eyes get used to the bright lights, I find two women struggling a few feet from me, one of them holding a knife. "A bit of help here?" says the one now pinned down by who I'm assuming was my attacker, so I shake off the shock and grab the woman's hand in which she's holding the small kitchen knife. I quickly force her to drop it, but before I do anything else she headbutts me and my mouth fills with blood. The bitch split my lip.

"Who sent you?" I ask and then punch her clean in the face while the girl who helped me holds her back. She tries to punch me back, but I dodge it and throw another one with a lot more force. "Stop playing with me and tell me who the fuck sent you!"

"What you're going to do me? Kill me? Go for it, that's where he wants you, anyway. Dead, or in here for life," she spits the blood to my feet and this time I throw her on the ground and use her as my punch bag until the other woman stops me.

"You don't want to end up in solitary. Let her go," she pleads with me, and through the fog that rage created around me. I stop and get up.

I wipe my chin of the dribbling blood. "You ever come close to me again, I won't kill you, but I'll make sure you wish I did."

She takes off as quickly as she came, and I grab the knife that's on the dirty floor before the other woman gets any ideas.

"Daamn, mama, remind me to never mess with you. I'm Jess by the way," she presents herself with an extended hand, but I can't ignore the irony, so I groan in response. "Something wrong?"

"Of course, something's wrong. Someone just tried to kill me!" I shout and punch the wall in front of me, pain searing from my wrist up my arm.

I grab my clothes and throw them on as quickly as I've taken them off when a woman's voice interrupts us. "Reeves, you have a visitor. Let's go."

Shit, this might be my lawyer. "See you around, Jess."

I follow the guardian through the halls until we reach the visitor's hall, and another guard gives me a number. When I enter the loud room, I look around for the number 18, and a face I never could've dreamed of seeing today greets me. I clench my jaw tight and try to walk over silently without making a scene. I sit down in front of the man and grab the sides of the table until my knuckles turn white.

"Don't make a scene," says the voice I dreamed about strangling for the past week, and although he's made some changes to his appearance, it's undeniable he's the same devil.

I take a deep breath. "You've got balls to show up here, Carter. You know they can't wait to get their hands on you, right? One word and you're never getting out of here."

Carter chuckles and sits back in his chair, which I've always read as a show of confidence and dominance. "I'm here to make you a proposition."

"You put me in here, so you can go fuck yourself and your proposition. Tell me what you did with my sister and why can't I reach her, you son of a bitch?" I whisper yell and bare my teeth like a wild animal.

"Oh, about that. I killed her. You've been texting me this whole time," he replies casually, and I feel the whole world crumble around me. This can't be real. He's bluffing. He wouldn't have done that. He knew her since she was 10. He can't be that heartless.

"You're lying!" I jump out of my chair and punch the metal table, making everyone look in our direction.

"Feel free to call the clinic," he says nonchalantly, and I want to rip his head off.

It can't be...

"You bastard! I'm going to kill you, you son of a bitch!" I shout through my hazy gaze and almost jump over the table to grab the fucker when a voice strikes from across the room. "Settle down table 18 or we're cutting it short!"

"Now, about that proposition," he starts but I

spit in his face and interrupt him. "You think you're the smartest one, but you always forget not to underestimate women, Carter! You think you're free? Well, enjoy your freedom, because I'm coming for you, and I don't mean that in the way you've been dreaming of for 10 years."

With that last word, I get up and head toward the exit. When I reach the guard, I lean in to tell him something while I glance at Carter because I know that'll just freak him out, but what I say to the guard is that I don't want any more visitors.

He approves my request because it's another one of my rights and takes me back to my cell, where I've been living for the past week, as Sean kept his word. When I'm back inside my cell, I'm stunned to find the girl from the shower on the bed above my own. "What the fuck are you doing here?"

"I've claimed a favor and got myself moved in. I hope you don't mind," she replies cheerfully and jumps out of the bed to stand in front of me.

"I do mind, Jess. It feels a bit stalkerish all of a sudden."

She rolls her eyes.

"I just got in a couple of days ago and took my time to analyze you and decide if I want to be friends with you."

"What if I don't wanna be friends with *you*?"

She rolls her eyes at me again and I want to smile but I decide against it. "Your loss then."

The word she uses strikes me like a bullet to

the chest and a million emotions whirl through me, knocking the air out of my lungs. Shock, disbelief, and overwhelming sorrow engulfed the very essence of my being, making it difficult to breathe. My sister is gone… my family, my everything… she's gone. I collapse next to the bed and use it to ground myself. I am faddily aware of Jess's voice trying to get to me but can't focus on anything else than the aching in my chest. Jess…

I take a trembling hand and press it on top of my breast, hoping to relieve some of the pressure that grabbed hold of me like a claw. A pair of arms wrap around me, and the touch alone makes me take a deep shaky breath. "Listen to my voice. Don't let the grief swallow you."

"He killed my sister," I whisper low, acknowledging the truth. The painful truth.

The girl nods and helps me get up on the bed while tears roll down my cheeks in a rapid fall. "He used me and then killed my sister."

"I'm so sorry, honey. It'll be okay. You're going to be okay," she soothes me, and I find myself falling into her embrace. I cling to her arms like my life depends on her embrace.

I don't know how long we've stayed like this, me crying and her soothing me, but when I finally feel a bit lighter, I take a deep breath and stop. That's the only time I allow myself to break down because I need to focus and think of my next steps. "I think he might've tried to kill you too," Jess says after a few long minutes of quiet.

It takes me 2 seconds to realize that she's absolutely right. The fucker did try to kill me, and he'll try again. With that, I suddenly become aware that we're not alone in this cell and turn my attention to the other 2 women who have been staring at us this entire time.

"If any of you get any idea to touch any one of us, I will make sure you spend the rest of your lives in here, got it?" I ask with a straight posture and confidence that I know none of them have, because, although I know they're not good people, I'm worse.

PART TWO
TWO YEARS LATER

TWENTY-EIGHT | NINA

"Gin," I say to the ladies and they all groan. I've been taking their money for the past 5 games and I'm sure they'll get tired of losing soon and stop playing with me.

They quickly pass me the 5-dollar bills promised and one of them quits. Soon after we start our 6th game, the door opens, and a guard shouts my name. "Reeves, you have a visitor."

"I thought I said no visitors," I snarl at the guard but don't bother to look at him or even get up.

"He insists he's family and that it's urgent," he

explains, and I get up with a heavy sigh. I throw Jess a quick look before I exit the cell and follow the guard down the hall toward the private interrogation room.

That's interesting.

They only take me to this room when someone important came by, so now my interest is truly piqued.

When we get to the room and he opens the door, I find that it's empty, so I proceed and sit down on the chair until this so-called lawyer or whoever he is shows up.

I study my horrible nails with boredom, hoping to send a clear message that I'm not interested.

It's only a minute before the door opens again and a beautiful man walks into the room. Time seems to momentarily pause and my breath hitches because his presence radiates a captivating confidence, and every step he takes exudes grace. With chiseled features, light brown eyes that hold a depth of mystery, and a smile that hints at a million of secrets, he effortlessly commands attention and he definitely has mine now.

The way the poor light contours his face makes me believe that beauty isn't just in his appearance; it's in the way he moves, the silent confidence that speaks volumes, making me gawk like a schoolgirl.

"It's a pleasure to finally meet you, Miss

Reeves," he speaks and unbuttons his grey suit jacket before taking the seat in front of me. It's in that minute that I wish I wasn't wearing this horrible orange jumpsuit because it makes me feel inferior, but somehow, I get the idea that whatever I wore, he still owned the room.

"And you are?" I ask with a raised brow.

He chuckles low and I swear something stirred deep inside my belly, but it could be because I'm so damn horny lately and there's no one to satisfy my needs with, beside my fingers.

"Oh, apologies. Where are my manners? My name is Damon Black and I'm here to deliver good news."

His voice seems familiar, but I can't quite bring that specific memory up, so I just shove it at the back of my mind. He makes it so fucking hard to focus and I find myself needing to clear my throat before speaking. "What could you possibly have to offer?"

I don't know how old he is, but that dark beard he's got is probably making him look older anyways. His tall and lean built makes it obvious that he's not just a lawyer, but I keep that thought to myself for now.

"Your freedom. You can be a free woman, Miss Reeves."

I don't react. I don't move a muscle, but I also don't think I'm breathing, and it's not because of the breathtaking man who's standing in front of me.

Freedom. I like that word.

"Let me guess, you want something in return," I say with as much boredom as I can muster and hide my curiosity and excitement.

Who is this guy anyway?

Damon tilts his head to the side for a second before replying, "I wouldn't be where I am today if I didn't have a few guys owing me a favor or two. I need you to help me find Brody Mason."

Can I be honest and say that hearing that name from a stranger's mouth shocked me or lie and pretend that I never heard that name in my life?

"What makes you think I know where Brody Mason is?" I ask with a raised brow and slowly wet my lips. But really, why do I wish that I looked my best for this guy?

What is this feeling that I have in the pit of my stomach?

Damon clasps his hands together on the table and my eyes land on his ring finger for the first time, and for some reason, I want to smile when I find it empty. "If you don't, you know how to find out. If you can't, then you know how to lure him out. You are the only person who Brody Mason will come running for."

Now it's becoming more and more obvious that this man wants Brody's head and has a personal vendetta against him. It's also obvious that he knows me too. "Who are you anyway?"

"Who I am means nothing to you, so let's not get into unnecessary details."

Now I'm losing interest, so I make sure he knows it. I lean back in my chair and cross my arms over my chest. "Look, Damon. I don't know who you think I am for him, but Brody Mason and I are nothing for each other. We're mere strangers now, so don't count on him showing up for a ghost of his past. If I remember him well, he ran from his ghosts."

Damon's piercing stare doesn't leave my own and under the light of the lamp that's hanging low from the ceiling, I can see how hazel they are. "I'm not counting on it. I'm willing to bet good money on it. 500 thousand to be more exact, and a favor a judge owed me."

It doesn't take long for me to understand that he means the price he paid for getting me out and that he wants me to know how much he's willing to risk for my help. For me to give this a try and deliver Brody to him, and finding Brody, could potentially mean that I can get to Carter too.

"And how do you plan to lure him out?"

"We're going to pretend we're dating for starters. That's bound to drive him mad and make him come out. You're going to live with me for a couple of days and I can promise you, he'll call you before the 48-hour mark. I am positive both he and his friend have eyes on you," he explains with ease and now it's my turn to frown. How does he know this?

"You're aware that even if this plan doesn't work because Brody Mason doesn't give a shit about anyone else other than himself, I will be a free woman? You can't take that back and how can I trust you on it?"

"I am a man of my word, Miss Reeves."

"Call me Nina, please. We're dating for Christ's sake," I say with a laugh, and that makes him smile. Somehow that makes me proud. "You've got yourself a deal."

He claps and gets up but doesn't proceed to leave. Instead, he places both his big palms on the table and leans in, pinning me down with his gaze and serious allure. "Just one thing, before I leave, Nina. I am not looking for Brody Mason to be best buddies. He has a debt to pay and it's time I collect. If you still have any kind of feelings for him and will try to jeopardize my plan, you'll go down with him. Are we clear?"

"The only feelings existing in my body right now are rage, hatred, and fury. I want to see them both burn. One for betraying me and the other for pretending to love me."

"Good," he smiles, pleased with my answer. "I will get things started then. Expect to be free within 2 days. See you on the other side, bella," he says before leaving and with that last word I understand that he's another one of Brody's Italian enemies.

TWENTY-NINE | DAMON

When I make it out of the prison and into the warm air of Denver, I have to take deep breaths to calm my racing heart and undo my tie to actually be able to breathe properly.

I've been dreaming of this day for two years, but I hated it. I hate seeing her in there and I knew it would be hard to look at her beautiful face without showing any emotion, but it was ten times harder than I imagined.

She's changed so fucking much.

Where she used to be a thick curvy girl, she's now about 3 sizes thinner and her green eyes have lost their fire. The eyes that bore on me with fierce threat the day we met, are now empty of all fight.

For two years I have dreamed of the moment when I could see her again and touch her, so now, being there, five feet from her, unable to do exactly that, was absolute torture, but I have to be patient.

And I know exactly who to hunt down for this.

"Fuuck!" I curse and kick a rock with my foot, trying to release the anger boiling inside of me.

I blow out another shuddered breath and take out my phone. I press the call button and bring it to my ear. "Steve, hi. Damon Black here. Please proceed and fill out the paperwork for Miss Reeves's release. I want her out as soon as possible."

I jump at the wheel of my car and drive off. I need to clear my head. I need to have a drink. I need so many things because the torture will end in two days, only for things to become worse when she finds out who I am.

But it's okay because I'd sacrifice anything and everything for her to be happy and healthy.

For her to be free.

I'd sacrifice my life for hers, that's how deep what I feel for her goes and she never even spoke to me before.

Some may call it obsession, but I call it soul mate. She's my fucking soul mate and she doesn't even know it. I didn't believe it in the beginning, but I knew it was impossible to lock eyes with someone and know that you're meant for each other.

My phone rings again and I frown when I see Steve's name appear on the display. I stop the car on the side of the road, a feeling of unease in the pit of my stomach.

"Mister Black, we have a problem," he says with a somber voice as soon as I take the call.

"What is it?" I grit out and get out of the car.

"The judge who owed you a favor and you were hoping to pass Miss Reeves's motion, has died of a heart attack this morning," he explains, and I can feel the blood drain from my face.

"Fuuck! Fuck, fuck!" I curse and hit the hood of my car with the palm of my hand.

This can't be fucking happening!

"Please tell me you have an idea, Steve, because she's coming out in two days, even if I have to sell my soul for it to happen, or burn down the fucking building," I shout in the middle of nowhere like a madman.

"I will figure it out, boss. Just give me a few hours," he pleads with me, and I have to blow out a deep breath, so I don't go and blow out the whole shit, Prison Break style.

"You have two!" I say with another curse and hang up.

She doesn't even know who I am, and I hate the prospect of her waiting for me in two days and me being unable to show my face there and give her the heartbreaking news.

***

It's been 1 hour and exactly 50 minutes since my phone call with Steve and I am glued to my phone hoping that he'll call soon. I've been glued to it every minute since I reached this motel close to the prison.

I have no idea what I'll do if he can't find a way to get her out. I might truly need to break her out, because one thing I know for sure and that's that she isn't spending another week in there.

She's coming out, and I'll be there for her when she does.

My phone rings in the next second and I jump up like my ass is on fire.

I answer the phone and immediately start pacing the room. "Give me good news, Steve."

"I have good news and bad news. I reached out to Sean Condreau, the detective who's been on her case when she was arrested, and he promised that she could walk free if she found Carter for them. They want Carter, not her."

I ponder onto Steve's words and although I know I should check with her first, I say, "Okay. Tell him that he'll get Carter if her record is going to be 100 percent clean. I'll be there in two days to pick her up, and then I can keep in contact with Condreau, but she can't find out, because something tells me she won't accept it. Thank you, Steve," I say and although I should be happy, this is not the ending I wanted, but it's okay.

It's just another reason for her to hate me, but that's fine. It's not the only one, so I can take it.

THIRTY | NINA

I return to my cell as instructed by the guard and quickly find Jess on her bed, so I gesture for her to come down and we both sit on mine.

"What's wrong?" she asks, concern filling her eyes.

"Nothing bad. It's good news actually. I'm getting out," I say with a smile and proceed to share with her everything I spoke with this Damon guy.

After saving my life, Jess has quickly become my best friend and my protégé. I made sure I had her back and she made sure to have mine at all times. There have been another two attempts on my life after the one that made us become friends but none of them were successful obviously or I wouldn't be here today, so we got closer and closer with each passing day.

In the two years that have passed, I had a lot of free time to consider what I wanted to do when I got out, but my goal never changed.

I don't have any friends on the outside, so I don't have any kind of information about Brody's whereabouts, but I know I can find him and finish this off.

I will make them pay, especially Carter. I will

do it for my sister. She was the innocent one in all of this, and I tried to protect her from this world, but in the end, she ended up paying for my mistakes, and my choices.

"What are you going to do?"

"I will hunt them both down," I reply in a heartbeat.

My goal has always been clear.

They cannot get away with what they did to me, and now that I have a backup, I am positive they won't.

Carter Stark will regret the day he saved me from that strip club!

"Can I look for you when I get out?" she asks with a sad smile.

"Of course, you can. I hope you do. I owe you a lot, you know."

Jess smiles and grabs my shoulders to pull me in a tight hug. I have come to love these. She does feel like the sister I lost, as my Jess sent her to guard me when she couldn't.

"Do you believe in destiny?" she asks all of a sudden, bringing a frown to my face.

I never considered faith or destiny. I never dared to hope that I have one.

"Should I?"

She huffs a breath. "I was at a fair once. One of those fancy carnivals in Mexico. I was drunk and probably high too, so I went in to get one of those readings. It never came to me until now that I remember the woman telling me she sees me taking the place of a sister. She said that I would one day call someone a sister because she lost a sister with my name. She said we'd be so close that we'd always find each other."

I don't know if I believe a word that scammer said, but I smile regardless because it's a beautiful coincidence and I do hope that no matter what, we'll find our way to each other.

"I always wanted to be a writer. Books mesmerized me and the possibilities that reading a book gave you brought butterflies in my belly. So, before my mom died, I used to dream I'd become a writer. Maybe even write about her. Then she passed away, I almost became a stripper, and who knows what could've been after that, and that dream faded away. So no, I don't believe in destiny because if I dare to believe in destiny, that means I have been dealt a really shitty hand, and I don't even know who to hate for it."

"Nina, you're 29 years old. Your life is just beginning, trust that," she almost scolds me.

"You sound like an old wise woman."

"Who knows, maybe I got to that point in a different life."

I always loved her witchy side. Her beliefs and naivety. I will forever love this woman like I loved my sister.

***

It's been two days since Damon's visit, and when the guardian opens the door and tells me that I'm free, tears well up in my eyes as if I've been told that I won the lottery. Jess jumps up and down and then hugs me and makes me join her in the jumping.

The guard laughs at us and tells me that I have 10 minutes to pack my shit, in these exact words. Good thing I have no shit to pack.

"I'll see you on the other side, yeah? Promise you'll look for me," I urge Jess and she nods her head.

"Promise me you'll stay alive, ok?"

"I promise," I say with a laugh and when the guard returns, I follow him through many hallways before we reach a desk, and they hand me my things. Which is my ID, my clothes from that day and my phone, no car keys, nothing else.

The whole process takes about ten minutes, to sign me out and all that, so when we get outside and I hear the gate's buzz, I almost squeal in excitement.

Somewhere deep down, I expect Damon to show up laughing at my naivety and telling me that it was all just a joke, but when the gate fully opens and gives me a good view of a black car with Damon leaning on it, I huff an unbelieving breath.

He's actually here.

"What took you so long? I thought you

changed your mind, and this was your way of telling me to go screw myself."

When he presses a hand to his chest and pretends to be hurt, I burst out laughing and almost want to hug him.

"That can still happen, and I will still be a free woman," I reply when I get closer, and he straightens up. He's wearing a black suit today and it's almost impossible to not notice the way it hugs his entire body, but especially his upper arms. When he lifts his hand to take off his glasses I almost gasp, but it could just be the fact that I hadn't gotten laid in 2 years.

"I like you," he says with a smirk, and I find myself wondering what he means by that. In what way does he like me?

"Can I ask for a favor?" I ask as soon as I get into the car.

"Anything," comes his quick reply and I almost feel compelled to test what anything means, but I play nice.

"Can you stop at a Diner? Prison food is not great."

"I'll do you one better. I'll take you shopping and then to a real dinner in the best restaurant Denver has. If you want, of course."

His suggestion leaves me speechless for a long minute before I agree to his plan, and we make our way into the busy streets of Denver. On the way there, my gaze keeps slipping to the way his upper arm flexes each time he switches gears.

"You a sports guy or just wanted a fast car?" I ask referring to his Lambo.

"A bit of both. I have driven many cars, but none impress me anymore. It's just meant to get me where I need to be, and I have a driver usually."

"Of course, you do," I mutter under my breath.

"What's that supposed to mean?" he asks with a huffed laugh.

I think long and hard if I should be honest or not. "Well, I never met a guy in such an expensive suit driving his own car."

"Have you met many guys in expensive suits?"

"Enough."

"Cryptic, I like it."

"I'm starting to think you have a crush on me, Damon Black."

"Would it be so bad if I did?"

I snap my head so fast in his direction that I get dizzy for a moment, but I decide to keep my mouth shut.

I decide that what goes through my mind right now is a bad idea.

A very very bad idea.

THIRTY-ONE | DAMON

"I forgot to mention a stipulation to my offer," I stop her before she enters the store and when she skeptically tilts her head on her shoulder, I smile in my head.

"What's the stipulation?" she asks, voice strained. I think I shouldn't have said it the way I did, but I couldn't stop myself. I love the way she likes to challenge me and how it makes me feel.

"I get to pick your dress," I reply with a smirk and wait for her to either slap or tell me to go to hell. Or both. She seems the type to even throw a good punch on occasion.

"Sounds like fun," she says with a wink, completely throwing me off, so I have to clear my throat.

I hold the door open for her and as soon as we make it inside, I watch her face light up as she takes in all the clothes and shoes. Women and fashion, I get it. I do have more than 100 suits after all. "You go into the showroom, and I'll bring the dresses I've picked."

"Wait a second, I thought you were just going to pick one."

"I will, after I see them on you," I say with a smirk and usher her toward the showroom.

I pick about a dozen dresses and take my time to imagine how she'd look in each one of them, although I know that reality will exceed my imagination.

When I first laid eyes on her, my breath caught in my throat and her beautiful green eyes had been stamped in my head for the past 2 years, but I couldn't get to her sooner, no matter how much I fought for it, and I have to admit.

I'm relieved that she doesn't remember me.

I shake my head slightly and make my way toward the showroom where she's waiting patiently.

"Ready?" I ask with a smile and when her eyes go wide, I can't contain my amusement anymore and burst out laughing.

"That's a lot of dresses."

"It'll just take you a few minutes to try them on," I place all the dresses in one dressing room and wait for her to enter it.

I sit on the sofa she was on and wait for her to try the dresses on, but she takes me by surprise completely when she strolls out in the first dress I picked, the red and very tight one.

"Can you zip me up?" she asks innocently, and I find myself swallowing before I get up to zip her dress. As I walk toward her, I can't help but notice all the ways this damn dress hugs her perfect body. I lick my dry lips and focus on bringing the zipper up, trying to ignore the way her lower back is curved. Trying to ignore how my mind is showing me all the ways I could grip that waist, right here, right now.

"Do you like it?" She asks, and when I raise my eyes, I find her watching me in the mirror, so I understand the unspoken question.

"It was made for you, Angel," I whisper and release my grip on the dress.

This was a very bad idea.

She proceeds to try and show off each dress, and I realize that she never asked me to zip her up again, so I can't stop but wonder if it's always been her plan or if she just didn't like me being that close.

"Which one should I pick?" she asks when she's done trying them all on.

I don't even try to hide my smile. "Oh, don't worry, we're getting them all."

"You were always planning to get them all?"

I nod and run a hand through my hair. "Of course. I just wanted to have some fun of my own."

She grabs a shoe that the store assistant brought for her and throws it at my head, taking me completely by surprise, but making me laugh wholeheartedly at the same time.

"I'm aiming again, stop laughing," she warns me, but I can't stop. I almost double over in laughter and trust me when I say that I haven't laughed like this in a very long time.

"Oh, come on, don't pretend you didn't enjoy it. I thought I'd lighten the mood a little with a bit of fun. Come on, we have to find someplace to stay for a couple of days and then we can go have dinner."

She narrows her eyes at me but doesn't say anything else. So, I grab the dresses and shoes for her, and we head to the register, where I pay for everything. After the assistant puts everything in bags, I take them before she can fight me and thank the young girl. "Sorry, we're not from around, do you happen to know a nice hotel we can stay at?"

"There's a dozen on them on this street but go find La Vue, it's two blocks on the left. They are the best," she replies with a warm smile, and we head out in that direction.

It's almost 30 degrees outside in the Colorado June air, so we rush toward the hotel the girl recommended to us. "What are you planning to do to Carter?"

"Braid his hair and sing him a lullaby. I'm gonna destroy anything he's built with my money, and then I'll hunt him down and put a bullet in his skull."

"I hate to admit it but that turns me on."

She winks at me, and I chuckle, but our conversation is cut short because we find the hotel and enter its lobby.

"Hello, we were wondering if you have any apartments available for a few nights."

"I'm sorry sir, unfortunately, we only have doubles left," the concierge replies, and I share a look with her, not knowing if she'd be okay with sharing a room with me.

She sighs. "It's fine, just get one of those. I'm starving and don't want to spend all afternoon looking for a hotel."

I nod in understanding and give my credit card to the man behind the desk. "How many nights should I charge?"

"Three?" I say it more as a question directed at the woman next to me and she shrugs. "Make it 5 nights, if we have to leave early so be it."

The man approves my request, charges my card, and hands us a key card. "It's room 24, right through that hallway, take a left and you'll find it."

I take the bags off the floor and we both head toward the direction we've been instructed to go in. We find the room rather quickly, so I open the door and gasp out loud when the room we've been given is a tad bit too small for me.

I don't like how small is the space we have to share and I'm sure she'll be just as uncomfortable as me, but it's a sacrifice we have to make. We can't go too far if we want Carter to be able to find us quickly.

"My bathrooms are bigger than this room," I try to light the tense mood as I set the bags on the bed.

Nina lets out a wheezed laugh. "Have you ever considered that your bathrooms might be too big?"

"Good point. Okay, I'll let you shower or whatever you feel the need to do, and I'll wait for you in the lobby."

"Sounds perfect," she replies with a smile, and I do just as I'd promised.

I'm also in dangerous need of a drink. A very big, very strong one, because this day is getting more and more complicated.

I sit at the bar and order myself a neat scotch when a blonde woman occupies the chair next to mine. "You look rather lonely, I'm Kath."

"Damon," I reply shortly, not sure why, because I don't want company, or better said, I don't want her company.

"Care to buy me a drink, Damon?"

"Are you a hooker?"

"Would it be so bad if I were?"

"Then no, I won't buy you a drink."

"Why? It sure doesn't look like you don't have the means."

"Because I don't want to entertain the idea that something will happen," I say plainly and return to my glass.

The woman scoffs. "You wish something would happen."

"I think you're confusing me with one of your cheap clients. I don't fuck out of need; I fuck out of desire. Now if you'd please excuse me," I say with a winning smile, my attention solely on the brunette with the killer legs. The dress she chose for tonight, is black, and simple, beautiful on her, but it's the way it hugs her figure that makes me gulp.

She's applied some light makeup and if I thought she was ravishing before, she is dead gorgeous now.

I just hope I don't have to bury anyone tonight.

"Am I interrupting?" she asks with an innocent smile.

I grab the small of her back and give her a similar smile. "You could never interrupt."

I lead Angel toward the lobby and once again, have to ask the concierge for directions. "What's the best restaurant this city has to offer?"

"L'assagino is quite good. Italian."

"Italian sounds divine," I hear Angel's reply and I can swear that her eyes sparkle.

"You'll need a car for that. Need any help with that?" he asks with a kind smile.

"That would be great," I reply and pass the man a 100-dollar bill as tips.

The car I picked Angel in earlier was a rental, so I just left it on the side of the road in a parking spot. She was right anyway; I hate driving myself. I'm surprised I remembered how it was done when I had a driver for the better part of my life.

I hate that she can read me so easily, but my father always said that driving is for peasants, not for kings and Capo's.

He used to say that if you show up in a Rolls Royce and you drive it yourself, that means you're driving for someone, but when you sit in the back, that commands power, wealth, and status.

I couldn't care less about any of that bullshit, but he wouldn't allow us to drive.

In the end, I had to go behind his back and take my driver's license, which up to this day, is still a secret.

I can't say that driving was a dream I had, but it is a necessity, so I had to do it and on top of that I was 19, of course I wasn't going to let my father tell me what I can and can't do.

THIRTY-TWO | NINA

The restaurant we'd been recommended is worth the status of the best one in the city and I can honestly say that just by the atmosphere inside. It's still quite early, so it's not very busy, making me grateful because I was never a fan of crowded places.

We ask for a private table and are seated in the corner of the restaurant, very close to the bar. Score!

If I'm going to be sleeping in the same bed with a stranger, I might as well be drunk.

Damon, however, is a proper gentleman and has been since the moment he picked me up from prison and I can't deny how surprised I am.

"I don't think I've mentioned how beautiful you look," the stranger complements me as soon as we take our seats. I might enjoy this fake dating stuff a little too much.

I smile, "Thank you. You picked it, remember?"

"I wasn't talking about the dress, although it's true. I do have great taste," he replies, making me laugh lightly.

I hate the effect he has on me.

I don't think there has been a moment today when I didn't have a smile on my face, or at least, in my eyes. He's just... so relaxed that he makes me feel at ease. It's like we've known each other forever.

The waiter returns with whatever wine Damon asked for and pours each of us a glass and another one brings us a big basket of fresh bread with olives.

"Thank you for this. I know it's part of the plan, but it feels good to be... never mind."

What I meant to say was... cherished. It's good to feel cherished but he can't know that. He won't care anyway. This is all for show for him. He believes that Carter's spies might lurk in the corners of the restaurant taking pictures of us, so he pretends to be the perfect date, and he is.

I can't believe that I'm going to say this, but Brody and I... we never had a chance at this kind of stuff, and I am wondering, would he be able to be so romantic and gentle when the sex we had was so chaotic.

Would we have worked in the real world when all of it was over?

"Forget about the plan, Angel. Enjoy this, we don't know how long it'll last," he murmurs and his left corner lifts slightly.

He is not wrong.

This beautiful, elegant bubble he has me in for the last few hours could burst at any moment. So that's what I do. I enjoy the wine; I enjoy the bread, and then whatever else he ordered for me. He's Italian so it felt right to let him choose.

What is it with me and Italian men?

It's after they've cleared the table that he gestures for me to lean in and when I do, although a bit confused, he tucks a strand of hair behind my ear and leans in, to whisper in my ear. "Don't look, but we're being watched and photographed. It looks like our plan is working. What do you say we give them some good pictures? Do you trust me?"

Good question.

Do I trust him?

He's done nothing so far to make me not trust him, so I nod slightly, anticipation buzzing on my skin, unsure of what he'll do.

What he does, takes me by surprise and takes my breath away at the same time. His lips brush over mine slowly, gently even, but I don't move a muscle.

I can't.

I'm frozen on the spot, and I let him take the lead and do whatever he feels necessary to guarantee our win.

He takes advantage of my silence and plunges his tongue inside, suddenly exploring my mouth. I don't want to react, but his mouth on mine feels too damn good to just stand by, so I follow his lead and do the exact same to him. We kiss passionately above the narrow table, his hands on my face, mine in his hair, hoping that this is enough for them.

Should I lie and say that I want him to stop?

Should I lie and say that my insides haven't heated up at the warmth of his mouth?

Should I lie and pretend to be disgusted by the way he's using me?

I can't!

I can't do any of that because this feels too good, and I haven't felt someone's lips in two years. I haven't felt someone's anything in two years, so I clench my thighs together.

"Our dessert should be here soon," I say as a pretense to pull away because any more of this and I might just straddle him right here.

"I got all the dessert I needed," he replies in a rasp, and I can bet my cheeks are pink.

He fucking made me blush.

"I hate you," I say with a laugh.

"Oh yeah? It turns me on," comes his whispered reply and I'm sure my mouth fell open.

How could it not? This man keeps surprising me, and yet, I know nothing about him. "Who are you?"

"You're not ready to know," he replies, his features darkening.

"Help me get ready. What is your relationship with Mason?"

"I can't tell you that or everything would go to shit."

"You're impossible," I reply with a groan just as our waiter places the tiramisu in front of me and the panna cotta in front of him.

"Impossible to hate, I know," he says and steals a spoon of my tiramisu.

"Tell me something about you instead then," I change the route. I'm going to get what I want to know one way or another.

He raises an eyebrow. "What do you want to know?"

"How old are you?"

"Thirty-two."

"Do you have any siblings?"

"No. It's always been just me."

I sit back in my chair. "Do you have a girlfriend? Wife? Kids?"

"If you want to ask me if I'm single there's easier ways than this interrogatory," he chuckles and tries very hard to hide his smile.

God, chin dimples will be the death of me, and I have to say that the short beard he has goes perfectly with his chiseled jawline.

"Yeah, but it wouldn't be as fun."

"You are not wrong about that. Any more questions?"

"Just one. Is the guy still there?"

He laughs, deep and vibrant this time. "No. He's been gone for a few minutes now."

"Do you think he's going to come?"

"I know I would. I would never let you slip through my fingers," he says with a hint of regret in his brown eyes.

I was never a fan of brown eyes, but I'm quickly becoming one.

"Funny, he said that once and then did the exact opposite," I say with a shudder.

"What's your story?" he asks and leaves me wondering how it is possible for a stranger to feel so familiar.

I sigh deeply and hide my face in my wine glass. "I fell in love. Isn't that how all bad movies start?"

"I think you meant to say romantic movies," he says with a wicked grin.

"There's nothing romantic about heartbreak. That's why I hoped I'd never fall for a guy, but I did. Fast, unexpectedly, and with the wrong person."

Damon shifts in his chair uncomfortably. "What else? How did you end up working for Stark?"

"Oh, we need more wine for that," I say and lift the empty glass, so he quickly calls the waiter over and orders one more bottle. "Stark found me in a strip club when I was 16. I was trying to get a job there because I had just lost my mom and I and my sister were all alone. I wasn't going to let my 11-year-old sister go into the system, so I had to do anything to make rent and food."

"What happened to your sister?" he asks after he clears his throat.

"He killed her," I say a minute later, a tear escaping my right eye.

"That's why you want revenge, not because he left you to rot in prison."

I nod. "He pretended to want what was best for her so that I did that job with them, but he killed her the minute I said yes and kept her phone to write to me. I… I never thought of calling her. I never called her…"

I fight hard to keep any tears from falling, but no matter how much I bat my eyelashes, they spill over, and I have to awkwardly hide my face with a napkin. "I'm sorry. This is embarrassing."

He grabs my wrist and pulls my napkin away so he can look me in the eyes. "This is anything else, but embarrassing, Angel. You have every right to grieve your sister and Carter… God, how I wish he were right here right now so I could rip his head off for being the reason tears cloud your eyes."

He then proceeds to take my hand in his and I melt from the kindness he shows me.

I can't help but remember how it was never like this between me and Brody and how I'd never seen anything wrong with it, but maybe that was because I didn't know how love should feel like.

I still don't.

THIRTY-THREE | DAMON

Seeing tears in her eyes makes me want to break someone's neck, but at the same time, I understand that she needs to grieve her sister.

I think she's doing something to me.

She makes me laugh; she makes me smile. She makes me want to be good for her but I'm okay for all of it.

I'm ready for all of it, for her.

"I have this compelling urge to wrap my arms around you," I say with honesty. I can't lie to her. She's had enough men in her life who all that they've done was lying.

"Could you?" she asks in a breath, and it takes the information a millisecond to reach me and then another one for me to jump on my feet, and as soon as she stands up, I do exactly as she asked. I wrap my arms tightly around her body and she lets her head fall onto my chest.

I keep her there for as much time as she needs, and when she wraps her arms around my torso, I understand that it'll be more than a few seconds, and I'm more than happy to keep her in my arms for hours if that'll make her feel a little bit better.

I'll pretend I'm doing this for her if that's what it takes for her not to run away from me because although my heart hurts, I know she will run away.

"Thank you," she whispers when she pulls away.

I nod and we sit back down, but I raise my head and gesture for the check to be brought up.

"You ready to get back?" I ask as I hand the waiter my credit card and the bill.

"Yeah," she whispers, and we both stand up and head for the exit as soon as my credit card has been returned.

"I have to be honest with you, Damon. This feels awfully wrong," she says as soon as we're in the safety and quietness of our hotel room.

"All good things do, Angel. I will sleep on the floor," I say and remove my suit jacket. I undo my cuffs and place them on the nightstand.

She feels the tension in the room because I hear her taking a deep breath. "Why do you keep calling me Angel?"

I ponder between telling her the truth and in inventing a lie.

I decide on the first option. "Because you have the face of an angel, and more importantly, because he most probably said your name every time he had you," I reply with a deep sigh and clench my jaw painfully, the image of the two of them together driving me insane.

"I hate it when you say stuff like that," she whispers and walks toward the window, and I watch her bite her thumb's fingernail.

I don't engage further because then I might become too honest and tell her how I feel about her.

How I felt for the past 2 years and how I've dreamed of her eyes, her lips... and her body.

"Everything okay?" I ask.

"I have this feeling that we're still being watched. I can't explain it," she replies and unfortunately, my mind does that thing where it would try anything to feel the taste of her lips again.

I start undoing my shirt slowly and walk over to where she's staying. "Maybe we should put on a show," I say low just as her gaze drops to my exposed chest. "Feel free to explore and enjoy."

She smiles awkwardly and when I expect her to slap me or just kiss me briefly as we did at the restaurant, but she completely throws me off when her palms lay flat on my chest and her eyes lock with mine in a daze.

"You're so hot," she says. "Warm. I meant warm," she adds quickly.

I huff a laugh. "You're hot too," I say. "Warm I meant," I continue.

"Why is it so easy to be around you?" she asks, mere inches away from me, our lips almost touching.

"Maybe we were meant to be."

"Kiss me, Damon. But do it like no one else is around us. Do it like no one's watching, like you really want to."

So that's exactly what I do.

I do what I've been absolutely dreaming about for two years.

I kiss her.

I crash my lips onto her and swallow the gasp she almost released. I plunge my tongue through her lips and taste the sweetness of her mouth. Just for a brief second before our tongues engage in a dominance fight and we start breathing heavily. I grab her back with both my arms and pull her closer.

I need her closer.

She immediately throws her hands into my hair and moans in my mouth, the sound driving me insane. "If you do that again, I might go out there, kill that guy and then come back in and fuck you like you've never been fucked before."

She swallows and takes a step back, quickly retracting her hands from my hair.

She also turns her back on me and draws the curtains closed. "We can't do any of that," she says when she's turned back to face me.

"I know, that's why I'm going to go take some air because I am a gentleman. And for the record, it's not because of what we need to do, it's because I don't think you're ready to let go just yet and I'm not ready to tell you the whole truth," I say with clenched teeth, mad at myself and exit the room before she can say anything else.

THIRTY-FOUR | NINA

I sit down on the bed and hug my body. It feels like history is repeating itself and I'm not sure I can do this one more time. I should have never given love a chance when I knew the outcome.

It's been more than an hour and Damon doesn't seem to want to return, so I sit in darkness and silence as his words haunt me.

Deja Fucking Vu. Another man who isn't who he says he is or who has too many secrets.

The door opens a while later and he walks in silently, probably trying not to wake me up.

"I'm up," I whisper and when he turns on the lights I gasp and curse under my breath. His right hand is completely bloody. "What did you do, Damon?"

"I punched a douche for having inappropriate pictures of you."

"What kind of pictures?" I ask as I head toward the bathroom to look for a first aid kit.

He winces when I return and grab his hand. "From when you were changing today."

"Motherfucker. I'm sure they don't need to see me naked, it's just his perverse curiosity."

"Exactly. That's why I punched him and told him that if I see him again, I'll make a hole in each kneecap before the one in his skull," he elaborates on his conversation, and I smile even though I shouldn't.

"It doesn't look like you do this often," I comment after I've made him sit on the bed so I can work on his hand.

He snickers. "The opposite, actually. I do it way too often. Torturing people is kind of my specialty."

I grab his hand and feel him tense under my touch, but I choose to ignore it. I clean it away with a wet towel and then apply some antibacterial cream on his raw skin.

"There's somewhere I have to go tomorrow, and I was hoping I could borrow some money," I say without looking him in the eyes. If there's something that I hate most in this world, it's asking for money.

"Hey. Look at me," he says, and I comply. "I'll withdraw some to make sure you never have to ask me, but I'm going with you," he continues leaving me speechless.

I clear my throat. "You don't even know where I'm going."

"I don't need to. You have my undivided attention."

I raise a brow, "There's someone I have to visit while I'm here. My birth father."

"The fucker left you?" he asks through gritted teeth, and while I'd like to think the reason is the pain on his knuckles, I doubt it.

I nod. "He did. I was 5 and my mom was pregnant. He needs to know what he missed, and Jess has the right for all her siblings to mourn her loss. She was a light for this world."

"So, she never met him?"

"Never... he skipped on us when mom was around 7 months pregnant. I was there when her water broke, I called the ambulance that Jess was delivered in and I was the one to hold Mom's hand when she passed," I remember. "But it's better this way. She never felt the loss, just the yearning."

"I'm sorry for your losses. You didn't deserve all that pain, angel," he whispers, voice soft.

I clear my throat to push away the tears. "All done, we should get some sleep."

Damon nods and I put the first aid kit away before jumping into bed. It then dawns on me that he's bought nothing for him today and he has to sleep in his suit, which I'm sure is not very comfortable when there's 30 degrees outside, even with the aircon.

I'll probably regret this later, "Listen, Damon, I think we're both adults and can act accordingly. I don't mind if you sleep in your underwear if that's more comfortable for you. We can put a pillow between us to make sure nothing inappropriate happens."

"That's very nice of you to offer," he scoffs softly and proceeds to take his clothes off while I try really hard not to stare.

Really, really hard.

***

I open my eyes slowly, coming out of sleep, just to find myself draped all over Damon's body and his arm under my head. Following my trail of sight, I also catch a glimpse of his huge erection, so I jump out of the bed like a snake has crawled up my leg, actually landing on my ass with a loud thud. "Shit!"

Damon follows suit and is instantly on his feet asking who's there.

"It's just me," I groan from the floor, still rubbing my ass cheek.

"Did you sleep there?" he asks, a sleepy frown of his face. I tilt my head.

How can he look so beautiful in the morning is beyond me.

"No, asshole. I fell out of bed," I snarl and get up.

"Oh, that was you? I thought there was an earthquake."

"Are you saying that I'm fat?"

"I would never insult your Goddess body like that. Room service?"

"Yeah, sure, wash away your sins."

Damon laughs at me and proceeds to order room service while I get a nice view of his ass. Goddamn, that's a nice ass. "Is it possible you could send someone out to buy me a nice-looking suit and some underwear please?"

His request leaves my mouth hanging because I never knew they did that and then he mentions a hefty bonus and it makes sense.

"How much money do you have?"

"I don't know, never counted them. A lot I think," he replies sheepishly, so I roll my eyes at him.

He's lying, I can tell.

"How did I end up sprawled on top of you?"

"You're so inquisitive today, Angel. You probably wanted a good snuggle."

"How can I be sure you didn't lure me there?"

"With what, my body heat?"

"Asshole. Why do you call me Angel, anyway?"

"Because I can't stand the fact that your name was on his lips," he says in all seriousness.

"A lot of body parts were on his lips too," I tease him, unknowing what a storm it'll stir.

He growls and after two long strolls, he grabs my waist before I get to process. "Do you want me to erase every trace of him, Angel? Cause I will," he says and nibs at my neck.

I want nothing more than I want him, hot and heavy, but he's right. He seems to always be right.

I'm not ready for him, until I let Brody go and until he tells me who he is, not just small bits of the truth.

I shake my head, unable to utter the words and he lets go of his hold on me.

"We've been together for less than 24 hours,

and I feel so free and safe with you. I'm becoming a different person. I can't get my heart broken again, Damon."

Damon doesn't say anything, so that leaves me simmering in my thoughts. It's probably because he knows that he'll do exactly that and there's nothing we can do to stop it.

But I... I don't feel different only, I'm enjoying it too. My heart is not full of rage anymore and revenge is not in my forethought. I want Carter to pay, but that's not the most important thing in my life anymore, it feels almost as if I'm excited to find Brody, just so that Damon can tell me the whole truth about who he is.

THIRTY-FIVE | NINA

It's around 11AM and I'm standing on the front porch of my birth father's house. A million emotions in my stomach when I push the doorbell. Thankfully, it's not David Bloomberg who opens the door, I think it's one of his kids, a 12ish-year-old blonde boy.

"Can I help you?" he asks politely but not polite enough for me to like him, or maybe it's just resentment that he had a father, and I didn't.

I clear my throat. "Yes. Hi. I think I'm looking for your dad, David?"

"Hang on a second. I'll go get him for you," he replies with a sweet smile and runs inside calling for his dad, but only after he closes the door.

I wait patiently, feeling Damon's stare on my back from the car, and even if I didn't thank him, I am so fucking grateful he's here with me right now.

The door opens, and the faint memory I have of him comes crashing down because he looks so different from the man I used to know. However, that man was a drunk, and this one wore a polo t-shirt.

"Can I help you?" he says, not recognizing me anymore. I was hoping he'd recognize me and make this easier, but I guess that's not the case.

"I'm... Nina Reeves," I whisper the name that should mean something to him.

I don't have his name because they were never married, but I'm sure that even for him, his oldest daughter's first name and his ex's last name should mean something for him. "Oh, my. Should we go somewhere private to talk?"

I think long about his question and agree only because I wouldn't want a young boy to hear me swear at his father. "Sure."

"I notice you're not alone, if you both follow me, I'll drive to a quiet café."

I nod and walk to our car where Damon is already out. "Did he send you packing?" he snarls, and I have to place my hand on his chest before he runs off to kill the guy.

"No, no. We're going to drive to a café."

He relaxes and we both get in the back seat of the car and instruct the driver to follow David.

"How are you feeling?" he whispers in my ear, his voice sending electricity all over my body.

I blow out a breath. "I don't know. Like I shouldn't be here. I don't fit in with his beautiful perfect life."

"Too bad he looks like he's a good guy otherwise I would've had a different type of conversation with him," he tries to cheer me up and it's working. I manage to crack a weak smile.

We reach the café in less than 10 minutes and before I exist the car, Damon grabs my wrist. "Do you want me to wait in the car or to sit at a different table?"

I analyze his beautiful eyes for a second, not knowing what to answer. "I would love it if you were there with me. I don't think I can do this alone."

"Of, course, whatever you want."

We then both exit the car and head inside the café where I spot David sitting at a private table in the corner, so I grab Damon's hand like it's something usual and head in the man's direction.

"I didn't know if you drink coffee," he says after I've taken a seat in front of him.

"I'll get it," Damon offers, and I nod with a thankful smile, although being left alone in the awkward silence wasn't the best idea.

I blow out a deep breath to calm my nerves. "I'm not here to ask for money or to be part of your life, so you can relax," I say quickly, hoping that would ease the tension a little bit.

Something passes in David's eyes, but I can't quite read it. I'm not that good with feelings myself.

"I wouldn't mind any of those two things, sweetheart," he says softly just as Damon brings in our coffees and I take a long sip just to bury my face in the mug and avoid eye contact. "But I know you don't need any of those things. Is this about Jess?" he asks and the fact that he says his name like he knew her close makes my blood boil in my veins.

"Jess? What, you were close?" I ask through gritted teeth.

"I'm sorry, Nina. I told her she needed to tell you, but she didn't want to hurt your feelings. I've known Jess since she was fifteen. She used to spend most of the holidays with us when you were…" he doesn't finish the sentence, but I'm aware of what he's implying.

I take a deep breath in so I don't set off, but I can't say that this hasn't shocked me.

Jess has been seeing our father and kept it a secret from me.

"She kept in contact with you?" I manage to say in a cracked voice.

"She… she came to yell at me. She was so furious, I have to admit, she looked a lot like you, but as soon as she saw her younger sister, Sarah, and her brother James, she melted. Just like that, she was a different person, and when I invited her in to meet them, she was surprised and eager to. She hasn't expected me to be a good man and I understand. I really do, Nina, but I've changed. Truth is, and I'm not saying this to make you hate your mother because she did what was best for you at the time, but she's the one that kicked me out, I never left you."

His words hit me like a knife to the gut, and I go back and replay each word in my mind, to make sure I heard it all correctly.

"That can't be true," I whisper and stare him

down.

"It is sweetheart. It is, but I don't blame her, so I beg you to not do it either. I wouldn't be the man that I am today if she didn't throw me to the curb."

His words seem sincere, but I keep searching his face for any sign of a lie.

"But you couldn't be this man for us," I utter.

"I... I couldn't. I wish things were different, but I couldn't..."

I bite my tongue hard to keep the tears from spilling.

"Here I was thinking you needed to know that your daughter is gone."

He sighs deeply. "I know. I've visited her a couple of times before the cancer took her..."

Yeah, the cancer.

"I came to visit you too, to deliver the news myself, but was told you didn't accept visitors."

Fuck me!

He delivers blow after blow. This man has known about my whereabouts for a lot longer than I've known about his and I'm not sure how I feel about that.

***

"I buried her here, so I can visit because I didn't know if you..." he doesn't finish the sentence and somehow, I know what he meant to say... again.

"You... buried her here? I can visit her..."

"Of course, I did, and of course you can. Amanda, my wife gets her fresh flowers every week," he adds, and a tear escapes from the corner of his right eye.

My sister is so close... I can ask for her forgiveness.

Why is this man so good? Why is he making it so hard to hate him?

I've never had good men in my life before.

Feeling the battle inside my head, Damon places his big hand on top of mine and continues to be quiet but attentive.

I wipe the tears on my cheeks. "You're making it really hard to hate you, you know that?"

"My bad," he says with a tiny smile.

"I... David, I don't know what to say. I don't know if I can forgive you for leaving us. I need to think, but I would like to see Jess's grave if possible."

"I understand, Nina. I really do. Jess was 15 when came to see me, but you're an adult. I can't expect the walk you down the aisle or for your boyfriend to ask for your hand from me. If you ever want to meet your half-siblings, just know that you're always welcome. Shall we go to the cemetery then?"

"That would be great," I say eagerly, and we all get up.

Damon follows me silently and once again we jump on the back seats of the rented car.

"You okay, Angel?"

"I'm confused, I guess," I reply, and Damon takes my hand once again, but this time, he takes it to his lips and kisses the fingertips, sending shivers down my spine.

"Do you want to know what I'm thinking?"

"Do I?"

He laughs softly. "I'm going to tell you either way. I think you don't want to give yourself the heartbreak of meeting his kids because you're not sure how this plan will end. Can I share a secret with you?"

"I've been asking for those since I met you, so yeah, please," I say sarcastically.

"I'm in the same situation as you. I can't let myself treat you how I want to because I know that when you find out who I am, you're going to hate me."

"Who says I don't hate you now?" I reply playfully because I don't want to ask him how he wants to treat me.

"You're impossible."

"I feel like I've lived a few months in a day," I whisper in defeat.

"I've been told I have that effect on people."

I gawk at him and narrow my eyes. "That you help speed their aging? I bet."

We spend the rest of the ride in silence and when we arrive at the cemetery, I thank Steve and promise we'll be quick.

"I think I'd like to do this bit alone if you don't

mind."

"Of course, Angel. I'll be close by," he replies and surprises me with a kiss on my forehead.

I follow David through the cemetery and when I catch a glimpse of my sister's beautiful name, Jessica Marie Reeves, I freeze in my steps.

I cannot do this... no, no no.

"Can I do this alone?" I ask David and he leaves me alone for the rest of the way.

My eyes don't leave Jess's beautiful black stone for the rest of the way to it and my heart already lunches in my throat.

"Hi, Monkey Face," I whisper, tears already welling up in my eyes. "I miss you, so so much, sis."

I touch the smooth surface of the stone and with tears going down my cheeks in furious waves, I place a kiss on my fingertips and then on the name written on the stone.

"I am so sorry for what I've done to you. I started this as a way to save you and I ended up being the one that got you killed. Please forgive me... Please, Jess," I whisper between sobs and hug my body with my arms. "I will never forgive myself, but I need your forgiveness to be able to survive this."

I exhale with a shaky breath and fall onto my knees. "Please, monkey," I whisper with a broken soul, tears streaming down my face like a river. I place my face in my palms as a sob rips through my body. And then another, and another.

A pained scream tickles at the end of my throat, so I don't think about it, I just release it, because everything hurts. My heart and my soul are shattered because although I have two half-siblings, they'll never be able to fill the whole Jess left in my heart.

And maybe revenge won't make me feel lighter, but at least he'd pay for taking an innocent soul.

So, I let the sobs rip through my body and the screams take away my voice until two strong arms wrap around me from behind and he lets me use his body to fall on.

"I got you, Angel," I hear Damon's whisper and let my head fall onto his broad chest.

I didn't think I would ever hear someone say those words to me again, and I almost can't believe that the one who utters them is almost a complete stranger.

But I need them.

So, I accept them.

THIRTY-SIX | DAMON

It breaks my heart to see her like this, but it is part of the process, and I am happy for everything she's learned today, even if being the only person getting her attention has been the highlight of my life, I know she has enough love for everyone.

I also understand why she wants Carter to pay so badly, and not only because he deserves it, but also because Jess was her everything.

Jess was her light.

And she is mine.

In the 24 hours that we've spent together, she made me want to do better. To be better for her to love me, but I'm just not sure that when she learns the truth, she'll still want me. That's why I'm trying to be a gentleman most of the hours, and then the rest I just want to be selfish and keep her for myself.

So, I hold her.

I will hold her for as long as she needs. I will be the pillar of strength that she needs until she regains her own.

"Why are you so good to me? I don't deserve it," she breaks the silence but doesn't turn around.

I sigh and kiss her forehead before I reply. "I get

to decide what you do or don't deserve."

"Is David still here?" she asks and wipes her face.

"He is."

She raises onto her feet, so I follow suit and she gasps when she sees my ruined suit pants. "Oh, no, Damon. Those must be worth a fortune."

"You're worth a million times more," I reply with a hint of a smile, and when she takes me into a warm hug, although I'm fazed for a second, I don't hesitate to wrap my arms around her.

"Thank you," she whispers in my chest, and I just hug her tighter.

God, how much I love her, and she has no idea.

We start walking toward our car and find David right next to it waiting for us.

"I don't know what to say, David, but I can't thank you enough for being there for her," she speaks softly and even puts on a tiny sad smile.

"The love you have for each other, the love your mom thought you... I hope my children have that for one another."

Wow, this man is good. I wanted a reason to be able to break his leg if needed, but I almost feel sorry for him, that he's lost two daughters.

"I'm sure they will because they have you as a dad."

She has forgiven him even if she doesn't realize it yet.

A tear slashes David's cheek and I have to look

away and clench my jaw, trying to avoid my own issue surfacing.

"I hope I'll see you again, Nina," her dad whispers with hope.

"I hope so too," she replies and gives him another weak smile.

"Here's my card. If you ever need anything, call me," he adds and hands Angel a small business card.

They don't hug, but they're both open to giving their relationship a try, I can feel that in their body language.

So, this time they only smile and nod at each other before they each get in their cars, and I follow her in ours.

"I'm exhausted."

"I know, baby," I say softly, and she leans in to place her head on my shoulder.

We just pull on the highway when the rear windshield shatters behind us and we both dodge the rain of bullets. "What the fuck?!" I say and raise my head to take a peek, only to find a guy half out of the passenger seat of a hammer, pointing a gun at us.

"Stay down," It takes me a second to bring my own gun out and to wait for a good moment to shoot the fucker.

He continues to fire at us until he has to reload and that's my moment, so I place my knees firmly on the back seat, place my elbows on the top part, and take aim, shooting him in one clean shot.

"Damon," she releases a scream just as another car pulls next to ours and shoots the driver dead. The car begins to swerve and Angel jumps in between the seats to grab the wheel, but she misses it by 1 millimeter when they shoot both wheels and the car begins to swerve out of control. I just now realize that we're on a bridge and when the car behind us starts pushing us toward the edge of the tall bridge.

I start shooting toward their wheels this time and I get one wheel of the car on the left, and one of the cars behind but it's all too little too late because we plunge in the air and head straight for the blue water in a matter of seconds.

"Jump out, Angel. Jump now, if we stay here, we're going under with the car. Jump!" I shout and push the door open, then help Nina to my side and push her out, a second before I jump out as well, just as the car hits the water.

The plunge sends me a few good inches under the water but then I fight the pull and swim to the surface. I immediately search for Angel, but she's nowhere to be seen. Panic rises in my throat as I look around, so I take a deep breath and dive back under to look for her.

Although blue from the surface, this river is not the cleanest and it's hard to see anything. It's a few long excruciating seconds until I catch a glimpse of some bubbles and her red leather jacket, so I swim as fast as I can before I have to resurface for air and lose precious seconds.

Relief courses through me as I grab her waist and swim upwards toward the air because she's unconscious and I'm losing my mind.

I swim just as fast toward the shore and drag her along. "Stay with me, Angel. Stay with me, baby."

When we make it to the shore although it feels like forever it's only taken a minute or so of swimming, I lay her flat on her back and try to listen for any type of breathing, but nothing's coming out of her, so I start CPR.

I take my hands and start to push on her chest with a firm rhythm as people start to gather around us. "Open your eyes, Angel!"

I continue alternating between pushing my palms hard on her chest and breathing into her mouth. "Wake up, baby, we're not done yet," I whisper and continue the battle with the only entity I'll never accept taking her away from me.

Not now, not ever.

She's mine!

"Open your beautiful eyes, Angel. Do it for me. Jess can wait a little longer," I plead, and when she starts coughing out water a second later, I collapse next to her and release a laugh while tears start running down my cheeks.

She continues to gasp for air for a few long minutes.

"Don't ever scare me like that, Angel, please," I say in a broken whisper and swallow the fear that's lodged in my throat.

"I can't swim," she wheezes, and my mouth falls open.

"I got you," I repeat and help her up as I ignore every person around and my attention is solely on her. "Are you thinking what I'm thinking?"

"I'm thinking about food," she replies with a tired smirk, and we start walking toward the road, hoping to find a taxi.

I huff a laugh. "Of course, you are, but no. Those were sent by Carter and he's going to keep sending them."

"Let them come, next time we'll be ready."

I couldn't agree more. "I think it's time to go toy shopping."

"Ooh, can I get a BOB?" she asks, and I narrow my eyes, unaware of what or who this BOB is.

"What in the name of God is a BOB?"

"A battery-operated boyfriend."

"So you mean a vibrator."

"That's very old school," she scolds.

"You don't need BOB, Angel. I can take care of that," I snarl, mouth going dry and pressure building in my balls.

Shit!

THIRTY-SEVEN | BRODY

I stare out the window of the penthouse I reside in at the moment and take in the beautiful city we chose to invest our money in.

It was a tough call between Shanghai and Beijing, but we chose the latter for the beauty, yet slightly smaller population.

We also chose the biggest and most famous hotel and put both our money together to buy it, but I think the most important reason for which we chose Beijing, China, is because of their non-extradition with the U.S.

Carter sold the cars on the black market, and we got a whopping 125 million per car, which brought the total to 375 million, divided between the 5 of us, which brought each of us 75 million.

Bvlgari Hotel in Beijing wasn't for sale, but with a value of 63 million dollars, and an offer of 120 million, we are now the proud owners of this beauty.

After Nina was taken into custody, I went through a couple of weeks of rage, anger, and guilt. After a couple of weeks where I drowned myself in booze, Carter showed up with a bag of cash. As every person in my place would do, I punched him for 5 minutes straight until he was bloody, and when I finally got tired of it, we sat down and talked.

I could've taken the money and parted ways with him or taken his offer and owned the biggest and most luxurious hotel in the world, so of course I took the second option.

We both put 60 million each and after the deal was done, we were still left with 3 million to spend on whatever we wanted. So, I went a fulfilled a friend's promise when I knew she wouldn't be able to do it. I went to Romania, tracked down Christina's daughter, and paid for her treatments. I tried to do the same for Jess, Nina's sister but found out that she had passed away.

I also tried to visit Nina to tell her the news and be there if she needed me but found out she refused to see anyone. I tried again last year and will try again in a few weeks. I just want to see her once. One time, just to say how sorry I am and to make sure she believes that I didn't betray her and that I didn't do this for myself, but for the both of us. This hotel generates over 20 million in dividends a year and a quarter of that is hers.

"I thought you were in the States," Carter draws my attention as he steps out of the elevator, and I raise an eyebrow in question.

If we're partners, it doesn't mean that we have to be friends, so I don't treat him like one. "What gave you that impression?"

"Well, I assumed you knew that your sweetheart just got out a few days ago," he explains, and although I hoped my shock didn't show, I'm sure it did.

How can I not be shocked by such news?

Last I knew from my contact, she had gotten 5 years, so that's 3 years too early to be true unless she got another deal in the meantime. "How do you know that?"

"You don't honestly think that I haven't kept tabs on her. She's a threat. She'll always be a threat, Mason," he tries to rally me against her as he's been trying to do for the past 2 years. It's not gonna work though.

I love her. I'll always love her. "But guess whom she's cozying up to," he adds and hands me a stack of photos.

I take the photos and analyze each one. The first few are of her alone, and then when I find her kissing a man in a restaurant, I want to teleport there and hang the fucker.

And then they break apart and the man's face becomes clear. "Impossible."

A ghost.

A man we all killed.

My brother, Damiano is alive and he's going after my girl to get to me.

I throw away the photos with a loud curse and head for the bar. I grab two glasses and the most expensive bottle I own and pour us two half-filled glasses. "She's harmless, you'll see. We will give her a seat on the board, money, anything she wants because she deserves it and take care of my brother once more if needed."

"God, you are a lovesick fool. She's not coming for our money, Mason. She's coming for our heads, and she's got help."

"And who's to blame for that? You! You betrayed her when you could have chosen anyone else!"

"I couldn't have done that, and you know it! She was there. She stole the necklace, so she was the best scapegoat. Look where her sacrifice has gotten us," he explains, and I have to take a deep breath to control myself and not brawl with him again. We do that almost every time that we talk about Nina.

"I better go before I fuck you up again," I say and start making my way toward the elevator. I need to be on a flight as soon as possible and find her.

"Again? In your dreams, buddy," he laughs, but when I turn with a growl, he raises both his hands and apologizes.

I take my phone out from the suit jacket pocket and dial my assistant Emily. "I need a flight to Colorado as soon as possible. If you can't find a flight in the next 2 hours, call Chen and find out if his Jet is free."

"On it," it's all she replies, and I hang up. I jump into the elevator and ride it all the way to the lobby. Me and Carter both have a penthouse in our hotel and there are 3 more.

"I'm coming, baby," I whisper and get out of the hotel to take some air.

I need air because, for some reason, my heart has gone wild.

THIRTY-NINE | DAMON

"I think I saw my sister," she whispers, lost in her own thoughts and memories from a week ago when she almost died in that river.

"I bet you did. I told her you're mine for now," I reply, and something flashes in her green eyes.

I am so fucking grateful that our plan is taking longer than anticipated, because I got to spend all this time with her before it all goes to shit. We slept in the same bed, every morning going through the same routine, me waking up hard, her falling out of bed almost every day.

We had breakfast in the room and lunch and dinner out, while we acted like we're in love. Well, I for one didn't act, but she did a great job when someone was watching.

"She told me she forgives me and that I need to forgive myself because it's not my fault that I have a good heart and that I trusted Carter. She told me to let it go and live my life," she brings me out of my thoughts.

"She couldn't be more right," I say with a grin and stare at the ceiling.

We're both lying in bed, hoping that her phone will ping or ring soon with a message from my dear brother, so I can finally tell her the truth because this wait is killing me, and not being able to touch her... it's torture.

By mistake, our hands touch and it electrifies my senses. Our fingers start playing with one another and I find myself yearning for more, so I turn on my side to face her.

A minute later, she does the same.

"I think I like you, Damon," she whispers, her warm breath caressing my face.

"I think I'm in love with you, Angel," I say with a tiny smile and caress the side of her face. I don't think, I'm sure, but I can't tell her that.

"You're messing with me," she laughs, and when my face doesn't change and I don't say I'm joking, she jumps out of the bed and raises an accusing finger at me.

"I would never mess with you. It's the truth," I say with a shrug and place both palms under my hand, watching her fidget from one place to the other.

"You just want to get in my pants," she argues.

"I do, but I wouldn't say something like that to do it. And I promised I won't until you know everything."

"And when will that be?" she breathes and does the thing I love most about her. Bites the tip of her thumb's fingertips, her gaze burning mine.

A smile stretches across my lips. "Are you getting impatient for my cock, Angel?"

"I haven't felt something inside me for two years. I would get impatient for any dick," she replies playfully, and I narrow my eyes at her.

"You're playing with fire, bella," I growl and jump on my feet. I start walking slowly toward her, like a predator toward its prey, when her phone makes a noise that has us both still and stiff.

None of us moves a muscle for several minutes before she is the most courageous of the two and grabs her phone from the nightstand.

"What does it say?"

"It says, 'I'm in Denver, I need to see you, Nina. I'll wait for you at Angus Bar, on the 23rd. Please, please give me a chance to explain and apologize. 7 pm, I'm waiting for you, baby.'"

Thinking of her alone with him makes my blood boil, so I turn around and take in a deep breath. Fuck, my time is up.

It's like now I've forgotten everything he's done in the past, the fact that he killed our father and I want to skin him alive for touching her and breaking her heart.

I fill the space between us and take her face in my hands to make sure that each word reaches her beautiful head.

"I love you, Angel," Her body goes rigid, and her eyes go wide. "And I'm not joking. You'll understand how that's possible when you know the whole story but for now, whatever he tells you, please promise me that you'll hear me out and believe that I love you, because I've been in love with you for two years, and I've been seeing your eyes in my dreams every night. Just know that I'll lay my life before you if it comes to it before I let anything hurt you," I continue and place a chaste kiss on her soft lips, because deep down, I know I'll never have her because of the things I did in my past.

"Please, please, promise me, baby," I whisper and hold her stare.

"I... You make me feel things, Damon, but if you lied to me... now it's the time to tell me the truth," she whispers back, and I can see so many battles in her beautiful green eyes.

It breaks my fucking heart and there's nothing I can do. This was always meant to happen, and I always knew I'd lose her before I even had her.

And in the end, I don't deserve her anyway.

She deserves a good man, and that's not me.

"I can't. I just can't because it'll all go to shit, and if I want my freedom, if I want you and me to have a real chance, I have to deliver Brody to them."

"What got you so scared, Damon?"

I close my eyes. "Losing you, before I even had you."

She gasps and parts her lips.

Then she leans in and kisses me softly, and although it almost feels like a goodbye, I take it.

I grab the back of her head and press our lips together more firmly. "I fucking love you without knowing if you'll ever love me back, and I will gladly do it for the rest of my life, even when you'll hate me. Do you believe me?"

"Damon…"

"Tell me you believe me, Angel," I press on.

"I believe you," she breathes, and I release the breath I was holding onto.

"I'll be there tonight and when you know where to find Carter, you can give me the signal so I can snatch Brody. My team will be waiting for us outside and if you need help with Carter, I'll be there for you. I'll always be there for you," I say and step back because this is getting a lot harder.

I grab my suit jacket. "I'll leave you to get ready."

When I close the door behind me, I have to lean on it and take a deep breath, because tonight is the night and I'm not ready to let her go.

I will never be ready to let her go.

FORTY | NINA

Damon's statement surprised me and left me with more questions than answers, but I can't deny that there's something deep between us. There's something that feels so right that it makes me feel like we're meant to be.

Funny to think about that as I walk into the bar. It takes me a millisecond to know that his eyes have found me. Then it takes me another one to find him across the bar. I move between people with purpose and confidence, making sure that my heels are extra loud on the marble floor. When I reach him, I hold my head up high and clench my jaw.

"You came," it's all he says.

"You called," I answer, keeping my gaze blank of all emotion, hiding the battle inside my chest.

He smiles sadly and shows me to the chair next to his at the bar. "You changed your hair."

"A lot has changed since you last saw me," I reply without any hint of emotion, even though my heart screams in my chest. It hates the show I'm putting on.

"I can see it in your eyes."

The reunion is a collision of emotions, fueled by unresolved history and unhealed wounds. I'm torn between the ache of what once was and the reality of what had become. The uncomfortable silence speaks volumes, but none of us seem to know what to say.

"I'm so sorry, Nina. I wish things were different."

"You left me behind, lied, and betrayed me. I paid the price in that cell for two years, and you wish things were different? Well, I'll be damned!" I raise my voice and slam a palm onto the bar, drawing attention to us.

He averts his eyes, "Things got complicated. It wasn't personal, I just didn't handle things very well."

"Wasn't personal? I told you I loved you a few days before that!" I say and avert my gaze because I feel tears stinging my eyes. "I loved you, and you left me in there to rot!"

Brody takes my hand and before I get enough time to react, he takes to his lips and kisses it, making my breath hitch. "I never stopped loving you either, baby. I thought I'd lost you forever."

I retract my hand from his grip and stare him down. "You did, but not in the way you expected."

"I never wanted it to end this way, Nina," he says, regret filling his beautiful voice and eyes softening.

I lick my suddenly dry lips, swallow the lump that's lodged in my throat, and laugh. "End? Who says it ended? I'm just getting started, baby."

"So you want revenge? That's all? Can't we find another way? Start over? Nina, for the first time I'm free, you're free and we own a huge ass hotel. You can be a part of it if you just let it go."

Suddenly I'm having trouble believing the words leaving his mouth. He really thinks I'll just put it all behind me and move on with my life. That we can get together and be happy? That bastard

"Let it go? No, I'm not letting it go. You had your fun. Now it's my turn,"

"I can't change the past, but I want a future with you. I'd do anything to earn back your trust."

"Earn it? You think a few words will fix the years I lost? Why should I trust you now?"

"Because deep down, you know there's a part of us that never died, and revenge won't erase the love we shared. I'll spend a lifetime trying to make amends. I can't change the past, but I can shape our future."

"There is no future for us, Brody Mason. You made sure of that when you chose the win over me. Now tell me where Carter is and we can both be on our way," I grit through my teeth and keep my gaze hard.

"Is that why you became best buddies with my brother?" he asks, voice dripping in hate, and I have to replay his words twice to understand who he means.

"What are you talking about?"

I don't believe him one bit.

"After everything I told you about him. After everything he's done, you let him near you? He's using you, baby. He's done it before and he's doing it again!"

It can't be, even if it all makes perfect sense now.

"You son of a bitch! You stay away from her, do you hear me, Damiano?" Brody shouts when his brother, *Damon*, my Damon, stands tall in front of us.

In all his elegance and confidence, I see everything now. Everything he's been saying to me over the past few days has led to this moment, but can I trust him now?

I turn my attention on Damon and the apology that I read into his eyes, leaves me almost crumbling to the floor. I had a feeling that I'd seen those eyes before and now it all makes sense. The day I helped Brody escape his brother, when I opened the van, those eyes bore into me like knives. How could I be so blind and stupid to not remember something like this? And the voice... it's the same voice from the night at the cabin. He's Damiano.

"Damon... This is what you meant," I say while tears well up in my eyes.

"Damon?" Brody laughs at us, but I don't care enough to look his way. My eyes are completely focused on Damon.

I wish I was not affected by this, but I am

because I... I almost fucking fell into a Masoni trap all over again.

I can't deny what I feel for Damon and how much finding who he is hurts me but at the same time... I helped Brody escape him and blew up the car he was in, and he couldn't care less about it.

He kept saying how he's been in love with me for two years and that was the only moment he saw me...

"I'm sorry... Angel, I wish I could've told you, but if you let me explain," Damon starts but is interrupted by his brother.

"Angel?" Brody laughs again and both me and Damon shout in unison. "Brody shut the fuck up!"

"I can't do this, I need some air," I whisper and head outside, just as a group of men enter the bar. It doesn't take me long to figure that these are Damon's men and Brody will be taken away, because of a trap I set for him.

I push the door open and take in long breaths. I need to fill my lungs with air because I feel like I'm going to pass out any minute now.

Damon surprises me when he exits the bar and starts running to catch up with me. "Angel... hear me out, please."

FORTY-ONE | DAMON

She looks at me and I can see the battle that's happening in them. I can see that she doesn't know if she should trust me or not. "You're him."

I am him.

I am the devil that you tried to kill two years ago to save the man you loved, and you only managed to make me fall for you instead.

Your eyes have been the lifeline I needed to get through the pain. Your face, the face of an angel has been stuck on my mind for every waking minute of the day.

But I don't say any of that. "He needs to atone for his sins."

She laughs in my face. "What about your sins? You've done things yourself. You're guilty of his wife's death, then you say you fell for me. What about your sins, Damon?"

"I have been paying for my sins every single day for the past two years, Angel. I've been paying with pain so bad that nothing can compare with that, and I will continue to pay for my sins every day for the rest of my life that I have to spend without you. I admit it, I was in the wrong with Eva, but you are my fucking soul mate, Angel. I am so sure of it that I can ask the devil to take my soul right now if it's not true."

When I'm done talking, I reach for her, and she takes a step back, making me want to scream.

"You saved my life," she whispers without looking at me.

"Don't sound so surprised."

She chews on her bottom lip. "You got Eva killed."

I frown but let her go on.

"You got me out of prison," she adds.

I am confused. I don't think she's speaking to me.

"You used Brody to kill your father," she continues.

"Are you making a pros and cons list, Angel? Let me help you. First of all, I didn't use Brody in any way, that was his own doing. I don't want to be the Capo. I never did, so when he forfeited that right, it fell onto me. I don't want to kill Brody, but they might, however, what they decide it's their choice. This was the deal. I bring my brother back and get my freedom. I have done a lot of shitty things, horrible things, but falling for Eva wasn't one of them. My father killed her, not me, and I will never apologize for that."

Before I started talking, I had hoped that my explanations would help her out. Hoping it would help her see me differently because if up until 10 minutes ago I was Damon in her eyes, now I'm Damiano, the villain from Brody's stories. "I am not a good man, Angel. I wasn't one for a very long time but for you… for you, I want to be."

"Was any of it real or was it all just to get back at your brother?" she asks dryly.

"Don't you ever dare doubt my feelings for you. Please give me a chance to show it to you. I know… I know he hurt you. I know you can't trust me, but I beg you to at least think about it," I plead and almost fall on my knees in front of her. Tears in her eyes, she looks away from my face.

"I… I need time to process it all and think about it," she replies and leaves.

I watch her hail a cab and my heart squeezes painfully in my chest, but I have to pull myself together and go deal with my brother.

I walk back into the bar and find Brody enjoying another glass with my men surrounding him.

"You broke her, you fucking left her in pieces," I grit through my teeth, and I swear if we weren't in a bar full of people, I would blow his fucking brains out for that.

He laughs bitterly and stands up to face me. "Don't fucking pretend that you care about her!"

"I do care about her, more than you ever did by the looks of it," I spit at him, and he growls, but doesn't move a muscle because he knows not to do any wrong moves when he's surrounded.

"You have no idea what you're talking about or about what love feels like."

I stare at him dead in the eyes and take in all

the differences between us. We're nothing alike. Not physically, not mentally.

Nothing.

We take after our parents, each in their own way, and right now, I am so grateful for that because I would hate it if she would look at me and be reminded of him. I would never want to do that to her, so I am grateful.

"Look, Brody. You can't run away forever. At some point, you'll have to face the Capos, so be a grown man and come with me back to Italy. Don't make me force you," I level with him and wait patiently for his reply. When one doesn't come, I signal the guys to take him away. I have a hotel room waiting for him in the same place we stayed at.

"She'll never choose you. She still loves me," he shouts when he's being dragged to the car.

"She won't anymore when I fuck it out of her," I say with a smirk, my sole purpose to rile him up.

Now I have to find my girl.

FORTY-TWO | NINA

When Damon walks in, he seems surprised to find me in here, so I force a tiny smile on my face. I hate how things have changed in the past few hours and how I don't know how to act around him anymore.

"You're here," he croaks and takes off his suit jacket. He walks over the armchair and places his jacket on the back of it before he takes a seat.

"What did you do with him?" I ask in greeting and I can quickly read the surprise on his beautiful face.

I have to know. Maybe Damon could be my future, but Brody is my past and he has a debt to pay, and I need to know.

"He's next door," he replies with a gesture to the left, and now I'm the one surprised.

He walks closer to me, and I have to swallow the huge lump in my throat to be able to speak. "What's going to happen to him?"

"Do you care?" he asks with a clenched jaw and a smoldering gaze. It feels like he's looking for the answer in my soul.

"I need to find Carter," I reply vaguely.

"You didn't answer my question, Angel. Let me be clearer. Do you care about him? Do you want to save him again?" he adds and stands up, his jaw set and his brown gaze piercing mine.

I pinch my brows together and narrow my eyes at him. He's angry? He thinks he has a right to be angry?

Fuck him!

"Back off, Damon! You have no right to be mad at me," I shout back and jump on my feet to face him. I'm not very tall anyway but sitting down is like looking up to a giant.

"Do you still love him?" he chokes out, his brown eyes simmering with rage and hurt, and my heart twists painfully.

It shouldn't though. I shouldn't care. He used me just like his brother.

"I don't know!"

He flinches, like someone punched him in the gut, and takes a step back, away from me.

"The man who knew about Carter's plan. The man who let you go to jail, and who's now still friends with him. And you don't know?" he whispers the last bit, and it makes me feel small and stupid.

He's right. Brody has done all of those things and I shouldn't care anymore but we have history.

I thought I wouldn't care anymore but my stupid heart doesn't listen to me.

It never does and that's why I'm in this mess right now, because it always wants the worst for me. It always beats for the wrong person.

"It's not that simple, Damon... You say you love me but how can I trust you after the shit you pulled? You lied to me and kept me in the dark. How is that any different than what your brother did two years ago?"

"I am not my fucking brother, and don't you ever compare me with him or with what you had. You let me show you that you can trust me. You let me prove it to you, Angel..." he whispers so close to my lips, a shiver runs down my spine.

As I let tears cloud my vision and roll down on my cheeks, I take a step back when he reaches for me.

I can never trust any of them again.

"I can't be here right now," I whisper between sobs, turn on my heel and run.

Although I hear Damon calling my name behind me, I don't stop. I run out of the room and burst into Brody's, who I know is next door because there are two men standing outside the door.

"Did you ever love me?" I shout at him when he stands up, surprise written all over his face. He looks just as tired and exhausted as I feel.

"I did. I still do. I am so fucking sorry how everything went down, I swear, baby," he replies, and his right hand reaches for me, but I shudder away from him.

"You turned my world upside down and then left me. You are one selfish son of a bitch, you know that?" I grit out and angrily wipe my tears away. He doesn't deserve them, and now I see it clearly.

"And you think he's better than me?" he spits enraged, eyes filled with fire.

He has no fucking right and it's time he understood that.

"See. This is what I'm talking about, Brody. This isn't about him. It's about you and me," I manage in a broken whisper.

Brody huffs a laugh.

"Just admit it, Nina. You like Italian dick," he grits out and I'm so stunned by his words that it feels like a punch to the gut, but I get over it quickly as the fog lifts.

I draw my arm back, clench my fist tightly and punch the fucker straight in the face with all my force, throwing him back a few steps.

"You are one sorry son of a bitch; I hope you know that."

I leave him stunned to silence and return my room, where Damon's mouth drops open when he sees me holding my red hand.

"That hurt," I whimper, and he runs to the bathroom to bring out the first aid kit, just like I did last week.

"You punched him," he snickers.

"Hell yeah, I did," I smile back with triumph. He deserved it, but I'm out of practice and it hurts like a bitch.

"You came back here," he adds, eyes on my hand as he applies ointment.

Hmm. I did. But I also have nowhere else to go.

"You have no idea how hard this is for me, Angel. Hearing him say those things to you. Hearing my fucking soulmate say that she doesn't know if she still loves him. I hate my brother for knowing you in ways that I don't. Your scent, the way your skin tastes, the way you move..."

"Kiss me," I whisper, and he shivers.

He doesn't waste any time though. He takes my lips like he's been starving for them, and I completely lose my mind.

All the things he's said, the way he looks at me, the way he touches me, they all add to the madness and before I get to change my mind, I give him all I have. He grabs my ass and has me in his arms so quickly that my only choice is to wrap my legs around his strong waist.

Suddenly my back is on the wall, but I don't care because I know that he'd never let me fall. Deep down, I have this nagging feeling that this is right and that I'm doing what I'm supposed to do with who I'm supposed to be.

God, this man can kiss his way into a woman's pants, and I now realize that he's been holding back before. I moan eagerly in his mouth as his tongue swirls around mine.

"If you don't stop me now, Angel, I can't be held accountable for what I'm going to do to you next," he says panting and I grab the back of his head and kiss him hard.

"Don't you dare stop now, Damon," I hiss.

"Fuuck," he breathes and starts walking toward the bed with me still clinging to his waist.

Am I making a huge mistake? Probably.

Do I care? Fuck no, this feels too good.

FORTY-THREE | DAMON

I lay her flat on the bed and I kneel on the side, holding her heated gaze with mine. I've been dreaming about this moment for so long, that it almost feels unreal.

My cock twitches in my pants but now is not its time. I start undoing the buttons of my shirt while her eyes watch me intently. "Are you sure about this?"

This is her last chance to say no because if I get a taste of her, I will not be able to stop. She nods once and licks her bottom lip.

Done with the shirt, she scoots toward me and touches my ripped chest while I watch her face closely. God, she's beautiful.

Reaching down, I undo my pants and remove my cock from its cage. It's been hard this entire time and precum beads already wet the tip.

"Fuck, that's huge," she releases in a quick exhale, and I wish I could lie and say that did nothing to me, but my dick jumps every time it hears her lush voice, so I can't do that.

I smile knowingly, excitement making my skin buzz. I don't know what will happen after this, but I don't care. I can never back down now.

"You know, there's one thing he never got to

feel me do. He never got to feel my mouth wrapped around his cock," she whispers in the next second, and when she grips me with her right hand, I swear I might be in heaven. She then looks down at her hand, and her eyes widen in shock.

When she wraps her beautiful full lips around my dick, I say a silent prayer in my head, hoping that I won't come in the next 10 seconds. I tilt my head back and close my eyes for a second, enjoying the feel of that tongue around my shaft.

I moan loudly and a smile spreads across my lips just a second later because it just dawned upon me that he will hear her scream and that will be just a great fucking bonus.

I stop my thrusts into her beautiful mouth. "I need to feel you, Angel. I need to have you before I come. Fuuck, I don't have a condom," I curse and back away a step while she wipes the corners of her mouth.

"I don't care, I'm clean. Haven't been with anyone in years," she explains and I'm almost relieved.

"I'm clean too," I breathe out.

"Then get over here and fuck me already," she says in a lusting voice, and I get rid of my pants entirely.

Then I step closer to her and with our eyes on each other, I take her dress off. "I knew you'd look like a Goddess in this dress, and now I get to see you without it."

I kiss her and she smiles on my lips followed by a whimper when I lean down and insert two fingers inside her sweet cunt. I kiss her greedily while I work two fingers inside of her.

"I need more, Damon. I need you," she moans, and my cock twitches with anticipation of finally being inside her. I grab her thighs and bring her to the edge of the bed so I can have easier access to her pussy.

I lift her ass a little bit and watch the head of my cock push inside her folds. She releases a loud moan and her entire body shudders, so she has to grab a hold of me to steady herself. "You're so fucking tight, Angel and I fit you perfectly, baby."

Her tight pussy clenches around me and my breathing picks up. I start fucking her hard and deep.

She's not the only one who has forgotten how sex feels because I haven't been with a woman for a very long time. But this beautiful angel is so warm, and soft as I stretch her out, that I completely lose my mind.

"Why do you feel so fucking good, Damon?" she exhales as she meets my thrusts.

"Because you're fucking mine, Angel!" I pick up my pace and it doesn't take long before she gives up and comes all over my cock with loud moans, her breathing accelerating and her body shuddering against my chest. Her pussy clenches around me and it feels so good. Feeling my balls tighten, I shove all the way in once and then pull out completely and come all over her abdomen.

When I put a baby in her, it will be special, not a first-time quick fuck when we're both too horny to think straight.

"This was amazing," I lean in, and she whispers on my lips.

"Next time I'll take my sweet time with you, but today that just wasn't an option. You were too good, baby."

I stand up and head toward the bathroom. I grab a towel, run some warm water on it, and head back to where a very satisfied woman lays on the bed like a cat. I kneel once again and wipe away my semen.

"I look forward to it," she says and covers her body with the duvet.

FORTY-THREE | NINA

I watch Damon pulling his pants up and hiding that monstrosity that was inside of me just a minute ago and I swear that my pussy clenches at the memory.

I just slept with the man who wants my ex, dead, but he says he's been in love with me for two years.

Do I believe him? I don't know.

Do I want to run away from him? Fuck no!

If he says he's going to help me deal with Carter, then I'm going to take him up on that offer.

"If you keep looking at me like that, I might just tell the Capos to go fuck themselves while I fuck you. You are addictive, Angel," he whispers and sits on the bed next to me. He gestures for me to cuddle, so I do just that. I place my head on his chest and listen to his heartbeat.

"Are you ever going to call me by my name?" I ask quietly.

"Fuck no! You're always going to be my Angel," he laughs and kisses my forehead. I love it when he does that.

"Are you delivering him personally?" I change the topic.

PERFECT SCARS

He sighs deeply and his body tenses slightly. "I have to, baby. You can come with me; I promise I'll keep you safe."

"I can't, Damon. I have to get to Carter before he crawls into a hell hole, and I never find him again."

"Then we'll get to Carter first and go to Italy after, but I want you to come with me."

"Okay."

"Just like that?"

"Just like that."

He smiles sweetly and I smile right back.

"Should we go find out where the fucker is?" he asks me, and my brows pinch together.

"Are you sure you want to do this now after we just...?"

"Oh, now is perfect. I'd love nothing more than for him to know exactly how real this is."

"You mean you're giving me a chance?"

"The fuck was good, but not that good. I still need to think things through," I explain and although his jaw clenches and his eyes closes briefly, he nods as he picks up his suit.

I know that he also wants Brody to know he just fucked me and maybe I should feel guilty, but I don't. I made my choice, and it will never be him.

I don't know if Damon and I will be together, but it doesn't matter. Just because we slept together it doesn't mean anything.

So, I get up and put on a pair of jeans and

a t-shirt we bought while Damon puts on his suit shirt and then his suit jacket. Of course, he wouldn't stand in front of his brother in anything else than a perfectly tailored suit.

When we're both ready, Damon walks me to the door, opens and I walk in to find Brody sitting in the armchair, a bag of ice on his bottom split lip. "Nice," I hear Damon's whisper and giggle.

"Where is Carter?" I ask, ignoring the other 2 men in the room, and lean on the small dresser.

"Why would I tell you?"

"I thought you wanted to build a future," I raise a shoulder.

"After you just fucked him? No thank you," he snorts and burns a hole in my skull with his gaze.

Damon smirks and I smile sweetly at him before turning my attention back to Brody. I love how much he hates this. "I'm going to find him, Brody. With or without your help but I'd hate for these nice men to torture it out of you. Now, you said you own a hotel and I assume you own it together."

"I came to tell you about Jess," he whispers a second later and I'm pretty sure shock rolls over my face.

"You came to tell me that Carter killed Jess? Don't worry he beat you to it," I snort.

Now he's the one shocked and this just confuses me.

"What?" Brody jumps to his feet and takes a few steps in my direction, but Damon steps protectively in front of me.

"You think I'm going after Carter because he used me? Jesus, Brody, I thought you knew me better than this. He killed my sister as soon as I agreed to do the job and lied to me for weeks. I don't care about you, him, or the money. I just want to look him in the eye when I stab him, not do it behind his back like he did to me. So where is he?" I ask with barred teeth.

"He's in Beijing, we own a Bvlgari hotel there," he sighs. "Nina, I had no idea about your sister."

"Let me guess, you also don't know he tried to kill me twice in prison and once since I got out? He will never let me be, Brody. It's me or him."

"Tell me what you need me to do," he replies, and I hear Damon groan in response. I knew he's going to hate this.

"I need you to tell Carter that we met and that I moved on with my life and then help us get to him undetected."

"What? No! Fuck no!" I hear Damon's disapproval and now I'm the one to groan.

"Damon, think about it! If Carter doesn't hear from Brody, he'll send spies again and then he'll run off and hide if he smells anything," I argue, and while I know he doesn't agree with me 100%, I know he'll please me.

I know Damon enough by now to know that he's also very smart.

"Make the call, Brody," I say dryly and Brody nods curtly. He takes out his phone and dials

Carter's number on speaker.

"I thought she gutted you by now," comes the bastard's reply from the other line.

Brody locks eyes with me for a brief second. "No, she didn't, but she wasn't happy to see me either. She doesn't want anything to do with me anymore."

"Of course, she doesn't, your brother's cock is probably better," he laughs, and I hear Brody's teeth grit together.

He takes a deep breath. "I'm getting on a plane tomorrow. But Carter?"

"Yeah?"

"Call off your dogs. Nina wants nothing to do with us and I think it's time we put her behind us too. Let her be if you value our partnership and our friendship," he says from this side and the way he puts it down for Carter, I can't say it doesn't stir something inside me.

I avert my gaze and look out the window.

"I'll think about it until you get here," comes Carter's reply and he hangs up.

"There. Done. Now what?" Brody asks.

"Now I go to Beijing and do what needs to be done."

"What about me?"

"You're coming with us for the time being. I'll get the jet ready," Damon surprises me with his answer.

Fuck me. He had a jet nearby this entire time?

"I don't want to get involved in whatever

quarrel you two have, Brody," I say a beat later.

"You've done that the moment you let him stick his dick inside of you," he growls back and that's when out of nowhere Damon comes rushing between us and swings at his brother.

"You will never speak like that to her. Hell, I'll do you one better. You will never speak to her again!" he growls in his brother's face and pushes him back on the chair before he strolls off.

Fuck this!

How the fuck did I manage to get in between these two?

I tried to kill one of them and he fell in love with me, that's how!

FORTY-FOUR | NINA

"The jet is ready, Angel," Damon startles me. I look at him completely confused until I remember that we're supposed to leave for China. "It will all be over soon."

"Let's say I'm coming to Italy with you, then what?" I ask, voice hoarse.

Damon walks over and sits on the bed next to me, so I turn to look him in the eyes as he asks me, "What do you mean?"

"Where do I stand with you being a Capo, Damon?"

I realize that I refuse to call him by his real name, but it feels like this is our thing. He calls me Angel and I call him Damon.

"Angel, I don't want to be a Capo anymore, that's why I'm taking Brody back. That was my deal with the others. I find Brody and they decide who gets to be the Masoni Capo. We have uncles, cousins, I don't care. What I want is to build a life wherever you are. Wherever you want."

"You really mean that?" I ask, tears prickling in my eyes.

His brother ran away from his feelings for me because of his own needs. He put himself first most of the time and that just proves why we were never going to work.

"Of course, baby," he whispers and brushes his thumb over my bottom lip.

"Let's get this over with then," I say on his lips, and after a soft, slow, and short kiss, I start packing the few dresses and shoes that he bought for me. "You're not taking your suits?"

"No, I'll just get new ones. I ruined most of those anyway," he replies.

He watches me intently as I try to fit everything into a small bag and his stare makes me all jittery.

"Stop looking at me like that," I scold him, and he blows a kiss in my direction.

"Like what?" he asks, gaze all smoldering.

I never knew I had a thing for brown eyes.

"Like you're going to eat me for breakfast," I chuckle.

"Oh, there's no doubt that I'll do that, sweetheart, but I need you to myself when that happens."

I think I blush but hide my face anyway.

He doesn't need to know that the thought of him having me for breakfast turns my cheeks pink.

***

I don't mean to eavesdrop on Brody and Damon's conversation, but after all, it is a small plane.

"Listen, Brody, I want to put the past behind us. I'm going to ask them for a trial and if they agree to one, I will testify for you," I hear Damon say and my mouth falls open.

Holly shit!

There's trials in the Mafia?

"Why would I believe anything you say?"

"Because believe it or not, I've changed. She changed me and I don't mean in the few days I spent with her. When she saved you that day, she doesn't remember but she looked me in the eyes without any fear, and it felt like she looked in the depths of my soul. It felt as if a bond snapped in place, and I had to see her again. So, I recovered from the fire, and for two years I looked for ways to get her out and kneel for her, but then I realized that I couldn't do that until I had a way out for myself, without having to bring her into that rotted world we grew up in. So, I found a way. If I could deliver you, I could have my freedom. I was never supposed to be Capo, Brody. You were. You were trained your entire life for it and then it just got put on my shoulders. I wasn't meant to be the leader and that thought kept gnawing at me, keeping me for being a good Capo. So, if they pardon you, it's all yours because I never want to step foot in Italy again."

Damon's words reach a spot in my heart that I didn't know existed and tears start streaming on my cheeks. They're happy tears because I never believed anything like this would be possible. I never knew I could be a part of a love story so beautiful when my life has always been a chaos.

"You really love her. You really believe in all this soul mate bullshit," comes Brody's breathy and shoked reply.

"Well, that's your problem, brother. You don't."

"What if I say to hell with all and choose to fight for her?"

It wouldn't matter. I would rather run off and never see any of them again before I give Brody another chance.

"I will never fight over her, because then she'll be standing in the middle just as Eva once did. I would give her time and space to choose because I am not going to make the same mistakes again."

I walk in slowly and take both men in. "Do you mind if I have a moment?"

Damon nods and leaves us alone, although is very possible that he'll just do what I did a second ago and listen to our conversation, but I don't care.

"You heard that, didn't you?" Brody asks with a raised brow, and I take a seat on the chair Damon just vacated.

"I did."

"Do you believe him?"

"You don't?"

He rakes a hand through his hair. "I know him better than you do, Nina."

"I don't care, Brody. I'm not saying that there's

going to be something between me and him, or between us. I'm just confused right now, and I need time to sort through my thoughts, and I can't do that until I've dealt with Carter," I explain, and I can see the hurt in his eyes.

"I just want to see you happy," he replies and shifts in his chair. I rise on my feet to leave when Brody's words stop me in my tracks. "I went to Romania. Beautiful country."

"Why?" I breathe.

Brody scoots on further closer to me and wants to grab my hand, but I withdraw it before he gets to touch me.

"I knew of the promise you've made to Christina, so I went and fulfilled it for you."

"I would love to say that I didn't need you to go and do my deeds, but a child was saved, so I will thank you instead," I whisper each word slowly.

This took me by surprise, but I feel so much lighter now. I can't believe he did that for me.

I manage another weak smile and leave Brody alone in the sitting area.

FORTY-FIVE | NINA

"Let's get this over with," I whisper on the steps of Damon's jet and look up at the sky, hoping that Jess won't hate me for this.

I descend the steps and face both men. "Ready?"

"I should be the one asking you that."

"I've been dreaming of this moment for two years."

And with that, we head to the waiting car that Brody called for us and head for the hotel, where we know that we'll find Carter.

The small airstrip we landed on is apparently very close to the hotel they bought, so we made it there in under half an hour. When I exit the car, I can't help but gasp at the beauty and luxury of this hotel and feel sorry about the fact that I will blow it all up soon.

Flanked by the two brothers on each side, we head for Carter's penthouse elevator. Brody announced to us that they both have access to the security footage but at the same time, there's only one elevator, so there won't be enough time for him to escape if he spots us.

I am so excited about this moment that my skin is buzzing in excitement. We jump inside the metal box, and I press the P button, so the thing starts moving with great speed, directly to my enemy's territory. That thought instantly makes me check the cold metal of the gun behind my back and I draw it out.

"Whoa, you're not actually going to shoot him here, are you?" Brody asks in a grave tone.

"No, but he may shoot us, so I have to be ready," I reply dryly and we all tense when the elevator dings.

The doors open slowly and when we don't find anyone pointing a gun at us, I sigh in relief. What we do find is a very relaxed Carter, enjoying what looks like a cup of coffee. When he hears the elevator and turns to look in our direction, I see all the blood draining from his face.

Part of me was hoping that he'd act all brave, but it's so much more satisfying to watch his eyes switch from fear to sheer terror for a second as he takes us all in.

"Nina, I'm so happy to see you. I see Brody convinced you to join us," he speaks evenly and raises on his feet to greet us. He takes quick notice of the gun in my hand and stares me dead in the eyes.

"Cut the crap, Carter. We both know I'm not here to join you. I promised you I'd be coming for you, but I never dared to dream that it would happen so early." With a smile growing on my face, I walk slowly closer to him and enjoy how my presence makes him feel. "I want to look you in the eyes so you will be haunted by Jess's face for eternity."

"Do what you need to do, sweetie. Death doesn't scare me anymore. I've built the empire I needed to build. Everyone knows my name."

I laugh and pour myself a glass of whiskey. I take a big sip and bring the glass up to inspect the expensive stuff.

"I think you meant bought or stole because I'm pretty sure you never built a damn thing in your life. You mean this?" I ask gesturing around me. "Oh, sweetie. Did I forget to mention that I'll burn this down and make you watch?"

My eyes find Brody's and I know he didn't expect that.

"What? That wasn't part of the deal," Brody argues angrily.

Damon clasps a hand on Brody's shoulder to stop him from coming closer. "Relax, brother, you're going to Italy anyway. Why do you care?"

"How's Ashley, Carter?" I ask, my lips lifting in an arrogant grin.

Carter's face darkens. "How do you know that name?"

"Who's Ashley?" asks the blue-eyed man.

"Damon's done some digging on Carter, only to find out that he has a 7-year-old daughter, named Ashley, who lives in Canada with her mom. So, imagine my surprise when he found out that there is someone in this world who Carter cares more about than his life."

I keep my face empty of emotion, grave and cold.

"Nina, please. She's just a kid," he pleads with me, and I throw the glass I was holding at his head and then stalk over to where he just dodged it and punch him.

"My sister was just a kid!" I shout. "She never fell in love, Carter. She... she was my baby sister, and you never gave her a chance to fight. Why would I give you that?"

"I'll do anything," he begs while I just keep my face straight.

"I don't want anything from you, Carter Stark. I just want you to pay, but I would never stoop down to your level. I would never kill a child. I just want you to remember, that I know where they live and what they look like, and if I ever hear your name again, I will come for all of you, but I might start with them. You get to walk away because I need to take my sister's advice and let it go. Killing you won't bring her back, but don't think for a second that I won't put a bullet in your head if I ever see you again."

I stand tall and proud while Carter's eyes go wide in shock. He can't believe that I'm going to let him go, and honestly, neither can I.

But he's not worth it.

Not anymore.

"I am done hiding behind these perfect scars, Carter, and letting them control my actions."

Maybe if I hadn't been so close to death or maybe if I hadn't met Damon, I would've killed him, but now I have a new purpose.

"Think of this as me repaying you for saving me from that strip club of those years ago."

***

Damon grabs my hand in the elevator, and I find myself leaning in for a hug and he wraps his arms around me without a question. I think that letting Carter go was harder than killing him would have been.

"That was unexpected," he whispers in my hair.

"It came to me at the moment," I smile sweetly and release a heavy breath. "I need a holiday."

"Can we go to Italy now? I'm sick of seeing you two together."

"Actually, there's been a change of plans with that too. Ariano is coming to take you," Damon replies to his brother and something warm makes its way in my heart. "I don't want to leave you here, but I don't want to take you with me either, so I found another way," he adds for me and completely ignoring Brody's groan, I kiss Damon long and deep.

"So, this is it then? You both show up and turn

my life upside down," Brody sighs as we exit the elevator and take the private one toward his penthouse.

"Don't pretend that you don't want to be Capo, Brody. We both know that there's little to no chance they'll leave Cousin Antonio in charge. We both win in this situation. Your only mistake was that you ran, Brody, you never stayed to face the consequences, and deal with the repercussions."

"Just for the record, I'm not giving up on you until you tell me there is not one chance for us. You need to make your choice, Nina," Brody says as he steps out of the elevator and into his home.

I am so stunned by his words that I remain frozen on the spot for a very long time, and Damon waits for me in silence.

I take a deep breath and step into Brody's penthouse, appreciating the fact that Damon doesn't say anything about what his brother said. I don't even know what I'd say if he asked me.

What I do know is that Brody shouldn't have said that, so I walk toward him with purpose and shove into his chest. "I hate you, Brody! I'm trying so hard to not let it take over me, but I hate you! I want to hate you and then you come and say shit like this. You're coming and telling me that you saved Christina's daughter for me and that you'll fight for me. Where were you when I needed you two years ago, Brody? Why didn't you fight for me then?"

"Because I was stupid and selfish, but I've changed," he says softly and grabs me by my wrists to stop me from shoving him again.

"I can't do this right now," I whisper and run toward the elevator, ignoring Damon's pained voice as he calls my name.

I need a fucking drink.

They want me to choose? What if I choose neither?

What if I choose myself for once?

I hail a cab in the American way, and I ask for the closest bar where I can drown myself in booze and not think about the two hot men who want me to pick one of them.

When I arrive at the bar, I pay for the cab and enter the bar. I take a seat close to the bartender and ask for a Martini.

"You don't look like a Martini girl," she replies with good English, but her stereotyping me makes me frown.

"What makes you say that?"

"Well, for starters, you don't dress like one of those bimbos. You seem like a girl who can keep her scotch down. Should I go on?"

I cringe. "No, that's enough. You are right, but I wanted a change today."

"Boyfriend problems?"

"Boyfriends… I think," I correct her.

She whistles. "You think?"

"Well, one of them is my ex who's done some

pretty hurtful shit and one of them is his brother, who's been in love with me for two years and we finally slept together," I explain but realize that I haven't even scratched the surface, but it doesn't matter. After all, she's a stranger and I'm here to get drunk.

"Wow, you've got quite the love life. Who are you going to pick?"

"I don't know," I sigh.

"You know this won't help you, right? You need to face them and make your choice, or you'll never be happy. You want my opinion?" she asks, and I nod. "Leave the past where it belongs, in the past. Listen to what your heart wants, not who your mind wants to be grateful to."

Fuck me!

She's right. I am grateful.

I've only started being confused since Brody told me what he's done for my promise to Christina and that somehow made me see a glimpse of the man I used to know.

But he did that for himself, not for me.

I didn't ask him to do that.

"Thanks. I owe you big time. I've got to go now," I say quickly, throw some money on the counter and rush out.

FORTY-SIX | NINA

When I enter Brody's penthouse, I only hear two lines from their conversation. I hear Damon say, "She chose me long before you showed up."

And then Brody replies, "Did she?" and that's when they both notice me and while I lock eyes with Brody, Damon walks right past me like I'm not even there. He only throws me a long and pained glance, that completely shatters my heart.

He read everything wrong.

"You shouldn't have said that. You had no right. We're done, Brody. If I choose him or not, that's up to me, but I will never choose you. I did that once and look where it's gotten me," I shout at Brody and immediately run to catch up with Damon.

The rain is pouring but somehow it doesn't bother me. What bothers me is how easily Damon believed that I'd choose Brody over him.

That the past is more important than my present.

I could never choose Brody when my heart belongs to him. I've just become too blind to recognize what was right in front of me.

Or maybe I was just too scared to accept it.

I catch Damon just as he's about to jump into the backseat of his rented car. "Damon, wait!"

He turns around and his eyes darken in the moonlight. "He lied and you fell for it. I could never... I would never choose him again. It's normal to feel confused, Damon, but I wasn't confused about who to choose; I was just scared to be with you."

"I would never hurt you, you should know that," he says, still holding his umbrella while rain falls all over me, soaking me to my very bones, but I don't care.

I'm shaking, but I don't care.

"It's hard..." I start but he interrupts me.

"No, it's not. It's easy. It's so fucking easy. I love you so fucking much that it hurts... it physically hurts me to think of you with someone else. So no, it's not hard because I would die or rip my own heart out before I hurt you. I couldn't tell you the truth about who I was before I got to Brody, but I have always been honest about my feelings for you."

I stare at him, without realizing that with the rain falling on my cheeks, so are my tears. A sob escapes my lips and that's when Damon throws away the umbrella and with two rushed strolls, he envelops his protective arms around me. A minute later he pulls away but only to bring his big palms to cup my face and smash his lips onto mine.

The world fades away, leaving only the echo

of our racing heartbeats while I take everything from the kiss like my life depends on it.

His kiss is tender but curios. Passionate but paced and ignites things deep inside me that have been dormant for a very long time. There's nothing sexual or erotic about the way we kiss, just pure adoration and romance. Just pure love.

"We should probably go dry off," he laughs as soon as he leaves my lips and grabs my hand, so we head back inside the hotel but only after he places a short kiss on my forehead that makes butterflies swirl in my belly.

I never thought it was possible to get butterflies when you're closing in on 30.

We book a room for the night, and we head there to wind down.

Brody is being watched by Damon's men until that Ariano guy arrives and then we can do the last part of the plan and leave it all behind us.

A fresh start.

It sounds like we both need that really badly.

"Are you really going to blow it all up?" Damon asks as soon as he closes the door behind him.

This place is truly luxurious.

"Letting Carter live was all the mercy they deserve. I am really going to blow it all up, but how do we evacuate the guests and staff without raising suspicions?"

I take off my boots and jump on the bed, a heavy and exhausted sigh escaping my lips.

"You sound as exhausted as I feel, Angel," he

says as he starts removing the wet layers. I should probably do the same, but I can't move a muscle.

"You certainly don't look exhausted, Amore Mio," I reply with a cheeky grin as he takes his shirt off and I get a good view of his toned torso.

Damn, these Italian men!

"Mmm, someone learned some Italian, it's hot."

"Not as hot as you look with those pants hanging so low," I purr and stretch across the bed to touch his abs.

"I'm gonna go take a shower," comes his reply.

"Hey," I protest and run after him in the bathroom, where I find him butt naked, laughing his ass off.

God damn it. That's a beautiful ass.

And it's all mine!

This gorgeous Italian man is all mine.

What is it with me and Italian men?

FORTY-SEVEN | NINA

When I open my eyes, Damon is still sound asleep next to me, so that gives me enough time to gawk at his perfectly ripped abs and ask myself how he says that I'm a Goddess with my size 8 thighs and stomach. Don't get me wrong, I'm not insecure at all and I love my curves and my big boobs, but I just can't stop wondering why he fell for me.

Why has this brown eyed, dark haired, Roman statue of a man picked me to be his obsession?

My eyes go lower beyond his waist and immediately land on his huge morning erection, and my pussy clenches even when I had him in the shower, less than 7 hours ago and I can still feel him inside of me.

God, he hits so good and deep with that enormous cock that I almost drool at the memory, so I do something that I've never done before. I scoot closer and insert my hand inside his boxers. He quickly becomes alert and moans groggily, making my entire body heat up.

"Wake up, charming. You've been summoned," I whisper and place a soft kiss on his pink shaft before taking it all in my mouth.

"God, damn it, baby," he growls and slaps my

ass hard. Being so close to him his fingers quickly reach my drenched pussy and start working on my clit while I take him deep and slow into my mouth. "Come here," he croaks and grabs my ass with both hands before he instructs me to sit on his face.

He wants me to do a 69.

"I promised I'll eat you for breakfast, Angel," he whispers before he swiftly introduces his tongue inside my vagina for a brief second, and then starts to slide it between my folds.

I have to release his dick for a second to take some air and he bites my clit gently in warning, so I return to suck on my morning candy.

We do for a few minutes until I feel my orgasm creeping up and I jump off his face so quickly that he's left hanging and mouth all shiny, so he wipes off and frowns. "What's wrong?"

"I don't want to come on your face," I say with a grossed-out face.

"But baby, that's the best part," he scolds me and tries to catch me, but I dodge his hand.

"Fuck no, we're not there yet. I need your cock," I say with a head shake and straddle him. I take his cock in my hand and slowly insert it into my paradise.

The feel of him fully fitting me just drives my senses into overload and my entire body trembles and shivers at the feels. I start moving slowly and moaning, but Damon being the impatient fuck he is, he grabs my ass, lifts me up and thrusts me hard. Even though I'm on top, he still wants to dominate.

Italians.

"Yeah, baby, you want to come?" he asks, voice dripping with sex, and I moan and nod at the same time.

"I'm close, Damon," I release a breath and meet his thrusts so he can hit deeper, and when my pussy starts pulsing around his cock, he grabs my body and throws me onto my back. He then withdraws, leaving me bare and needy.

"Not just yet, bella. What's the rush?" he snorts and starts stoking his dick with one hand while the other comes up to my breasts. He is purposely ignoring my clit and that just makes me growl and I shove my hand forward to touch myself when he quickly grabs my wrist.

"Tsk, tsk, no touching, bella, or I'll have to tie you up."

His words surprise and excite me at the same time, and I think he can see it in my eyes because he inclines his head and a mischievous smile spreads on his lips.

"Do you want to be tied up, Angel?" he asks with a grin, and I nod shyly.

He gets off the bed in the next second and grabs a tie from his bag, the one he never actually used and comes back on the bed where I'm already touching myself. How can I not when he shows me that ass?

"I said no touching, Angel," he laughs and

grabs both my wrists and ties them together above my head. With him leaning to push them on top of my head, his dick slowly touches my clit, and my body goes haywire. "Please, Damon."

"What do you want, Angel?"

"I want you to fuck me into oblivion."

And with that, he does.

He's gentle and slow at first as he enters my soaked folds once again, but he quickly picks up the pace and reaches me deeper with each thrust.

The urge to touch him is so intense and the fact that I can't keep my senses in overload, so when he finally starts rubbing my clit, I burst like a million stars. My body starts convulsing while my pussy clenches around him like crazy and our moans and groans intertwine in the hot mess.

He changes the rhythm with each thrust, and I start writhing underneath him because although my nerves are on fire, I don't want him to stop.

"I'm coming, Angel," he roars and pushes two more times so deep that I know I will be sore for days, but when his semen fills me, it's a sensation I never felt before and a sensation that I know is going to be addictive.

Although I'm high on pleasure, I become more and more aware of the fact that he just released himself inside of me while I'm not on any birth control, but that's a problem that we can talk about a bit later because right now I just need to feel his body next to mine.

"Are you okay?" he asks after he's sat next to me, and I cuddle up against his steaming body.

"Now it's not the right time."

"Angel, tell me what's wrong?"

"I'm not on birth control, and we just…" but I don't finish the sentence because he stands up and swears.

"Oh, shit. Angel, I'm so sorry, I didn't realize. What do you need, I'll go get it for you," he says softly and kisses my shoulder.

"There's a morning-after pill that I can take to minimize the risks of an unwanted pregnancy," I explain and something weird passes in his brown eyes.

"There's no such thing as an unwanted baby. It'd be a happy accident, but not unwanted, okay? But this is entirely your choice," he assures me with soft eyes and my heart squeezes at the next thought.

He wants kids, but what if I don't?

"I'm not sure how I feel about having kids, Damon, so until I figure that out, I think the pill and some birth control would be a good idea."

What he might say next scares me, but I'm glad it came up before we invested too many feelings.

"Whatever you're comfortable with, but mark my words, Angel. You're going to love me so much one day, that you'll want me to put a baby in you."

"I hope you're right."

FORTY-EIGHT | DAMON

Although we are in a very big city in China, that doesn't mean that everyone speaks English, so when the old pharmacist doesn't understand what I'm asking about, I have to take my phone out and translate it for her. She looks at the phone, then frowns, then looks at me with a narrowed gaze. Only after she says something in Chinese does she go into the storage room to bring me what I need.

Just as I pay and take the product, my phone rings in my jacket and I take it out to answer. "Ariano, should I send a car for you?" I ask him in Italian.

"No need, I'm already at the hotel waiting for you."

"I'll be back in 5 minutes."

Ariano hangs up and I return to my car where the driver waits for me. When I make it back at the hotel, I find Ariano in the lobby with two other men and I keep my face unreadable.

"Fast and furious, I like it," I greet him.

"I don't waste my time like you do," the older man scolds me with a raised brow.

"I found him, haven't I? Let's go upstairs, I'll take you to him, but Ariano, I want you both gone before sundown,"

The man nods and I lead him toward the penthouse elevator. When we arrive upstairs and the doors open, I sigh in relief when I find Brody on the sofa. I know my brother well enough to know that if he wanted, he would've walked out of here.

"Ariano, welcome to China. I guess one of your fantasies came to life," Brody greets our old friend with a nasty grin making Ariano cringe.

"I've got somewhere to be, so it'd be best if you were on your way already. You can take the jet back and the men I guess, as I'm done being Capo," I say to the two men and Ariano nods.

I knew I'd have to give up on some things when I found Brody, but I am content with that. I don't need men and a jet when all I want is to settle down and open a small business. I have enough money on the side to last me and my kids lifetimes, but I know that I'll get bored quickly and come up with something new to do wherever we put down roots.

"So, are we done here?" I nudge again.

"Yeah, we're done. I'd rather be back in Italy before my wife gives birth, which should be any day now. Ready to go, Bruno?" he asks my brother, who locks eyes with me in a silent question.

But I don't have an answer for him.

The only person who can answer that is her. "I'll let her know. Wait in the lobby for 10 minutes. If she wants to say goodbye, I'll tell her to come down there."

Brody nods sadly and all men jump in the elevator. He takes nothing with him. No pictures, no clothes, nothing.

I look around me for a while until I hear the elevator becoming available again because I'll have to ride it downstairs, but I didn't want to be inside with them.

I know he'll be okay, but I spent so much time hunting him down, hating him, that I don't know how to be happy for him. I'll have to find a way I guess, because if I'm right and he's going to be the new Capo, we'll cross paths, I'm sure.

After all, he's the only family I have left.

On that thought, I jump in the elevator and ride it express all the way to the first floor, where our room is and when I enter it, I find Angel looking out the window lost in thought. "Hey, baby."

"Hey, you're back."

"I think you should know that Ariano is here for my brother, and they're leaving in about 10 minutes. I thought you might want to say goodbye."

Even though the last thing I want her to do it go downstairs and have a heart-to-heart goodbye with her ex, I will always be honest with her and give her the choice.

"I don't to, but thanks," she replies cheerfully and takes the box from my hand.

PERFECT SCARS

She takes out the pill and a bottle of water and quickly swallows it. "Are you sure, Angel?"

"Damon, I'm sure, I promise, and it has nothing to do with us. He just doesn't deserve it," she assures me and leans in for a kiss.

I smile on her plump lips. "I love you, Angel."

"I think I'm falling in love with you," she replies and my heart swells.

She loves me, but I can't accept her love until she knows everything.

"There's something else I have to tell you, baby. It's the only secret left, I swear it on my soul and my mother's grave. I had to make a deal with the feds for your release. They're waiting for Carter when he gets to Canada," I say and wait for her rage to show.

"I don't care. He deserves it," she whispers, and I can't fucking believe my ears.

"Are you sure?"

She nods, tears prickling in her eyes. "Never been surer in my life. I think you've proven yourself, Damiano," she adds my real name at the end and when my eyes become teary, she releases a strangled laugh. "I've made Damiano Masoni cry."

"I know, fucking pathetic," I reply and wipe the corners of my eyes with a smile.

It's like my craziest dream has come true, and maybe it has, or maybe this is all a dream.

Just don't wake me up.

"What are you thinking about?"

"I was thinking that if this is a dream, I hope no one dares to wake me up."

"That's very romantic of you, baby."

"Oh, you ain't seen nothing yet," I joke. "I think I might have an idea about how to empty this place of people."

"Yeah?"

"I think the safest and most unsuspicious way to make everyone run, would be a flea or bed bugs outbreak."

When Angel burst out laughing, I knew that my plans had worked. It was supposed to be funny because we won't do any of those two things.

We're going to do something that's never been heard of.

"Thanks for that, I need it," she says while she wipes away her tears, and I kiss her forehead when she calms down.

I take a set of papers out of my back pocket and hand it over to her. "Here's the real idea, Angel."

She takes the papers with a frown and opens them to read through the pages. When she's done, she closes the folder and looks me dead in the eyes with a stern look.

Oh shit!

"They signed it all over to me?! I don't want it, Damon," she whispers and sorrow fills her beautiful eyes.

I pull her to sit on the bed and take her hands in mine. "I know you don't, baby. But it's yours, so rather than burning it down, what do you say about selling it and donating the money to cancer research or wherever you want?"

FORTY-NINE | NINA

That's not possible, is it?

"Is that even possible? To donate that much money?" I ask, still stunned about his idea.

God, he's a good man.

"You can do whatever you want with your money. If an organization can't accept that much, then you share it with as many as you want. You don't have to keep a penny, and the market value is 70 million anyway, a lot less than what they've paid for it."

"That's just perfect, Damon. I can donate most of it to cancer research and cancer facilities and the rest, to orphan children. There are so many places I want to donate it to that it now just doesn't feel enough," I say in excitement and Damon has to place a hand on my knee to help me relax a bit.

How did I go from burning it down to hoping it sells for a good price so that I can help as many people as possible?

"It's a good thing that I had the lawyers draft some offers for you. They're my brother's lawyers, but for a hefty cut of the sale, they'll make sure it's a good deal," he explains, and I still cannot believe where we are and what we're about to do.

"How are you so perfect?"

"Because you make me want to be a better man," he replies and kisses me deeply. My heart skips a beat every time his lips touch mine and I will never get used to it.

But I love this man.

I love him deeply, and truly.

I know that it would be an all-consuming type of love, but sweetly and passionately, not chaotic and toxic.

"I want to get back to the States, I don't like this country. I mean the country is beautiful, I just hate to not be able to understand what people around me are saying," I laugh, and Damon agrees with me.

"Let's go have some early lunch and hopefully offers will start pouring in before we finish," he suggests, and I very much like his idea.

"You know what? We're in Beijing, China and who knows what tomorrow has in store for us. If I'm not completely wrong, we're about 2 hours from The Great Wall of China."

I'm suddenly excited again. I was so stuck on revenge and tearing this place apart that it never occurred to me how I've never been out of the States and this country is absolutely beautiful.

"Okay, let's be tourists for a day, but after lunch, because I'm not eating whatever insects they serve in that forest," he cringes and makes a gagging noise.

Damon calls the reception to get us a car and I start jumping in excitement. I don't know how this turned out this way, but I am beyond grateful, and without bragging too much, I think I've made some damn good choices.

"Ready, my Angel?" he asks and extends his open palm for me with a loving grin.

My heart skips a beat. "I'm ready, *Amore*."

FIFTY | ANGEL

Being a normal couple for a day, just two tourists in a sea of mostly Chinese people, was absolutely beautiful and it gave me a sense of normalcy that I think I'd lost when my mother died.

I never knew I missed it until I was reminded of it, and Damon, ex-Mafia Capo, a man who hunted his brother for over 5 years, if I remember correctly, is just a normal, charming man, making every one of my wishes come true.

He makes me fall in love with him a tad bit more each hour that we spend together.

A week's passed since our day trip to the Wall, and we've spent the entire time signing papers for the sale to go through. Yes, we received an offer of 73.5 million, which I took with a victorious smile.

I am now the proud owner of an account full of money that I've come to terms with the fact that they aren't mine, although… they are. It's more or less the amount they owed me for the job, and in the end, it found its way to me.

After the papers had been signed and the transaction made, we took a red eye back to Denver. When I asked Damon where he wanted to go, he told me, 'Let's go back to Denver, and take it from there?'

This time, we decided to skip the hotel and rent an Airbnb. We don't know how long we'll be here, but I'm done with living in a hotel.

In the silence and intimacy of our new temporary home, I ask the one question I haven't dared ask so far. "Damon... could you tell me about her? About everything?"

"Why?"

"I want to hear your side of things too," I whisper and take his hand in mine.

I've been cuddled up in his arms for more than an hour now because we've been watching a rom-com movie, so now I turn and look him in the eyes.

"I would like to say that I saw Eva first, but I didn't. Bruno met Eva at boarding school and when he brought her home one night, I instantly got a crush on her," and that's when I avert my eyes. "She kissed me. When he brought her home for the first time, she kissed me. She had this fantasy of doing her boyfriend's brother and keeping it a secret. I loved the idea, I was 17, horny as fuck, who wouldn't like some secret girlfriend."

"Oh my God."

"She liked to live in a fantasy, and we kept it up for a few years but when Brody said he wanted to marry her, things got complicated. I didn't love her, but I liked to bust his balls for it and the

PERFECT SCARS

fact that she wanted me too. He hated that idea, and we fought a lot because of it, although now that I think about it, I didn't want Eva, I just... I think I wanted someone better for him. Someone who wouldn't sneak into my bedroom after she'd had sex with him," he continues and I'm sure my mouth is open, and my eyes are wide.

"Does Brody... does he still not believe you?"

"I think he loved her too much, and he chose not to believe me," he says with a sad smile, and to some extent, I believe he's right.

I think so too. Brody was blinded by his first love and that's completely normal.

"What she's done... was terrible and she got what she deserved. I'm just sorry that her death started a series of even worse events," I whisper, voice filled with anger toward the woman who ruined two lives.

"Forget about her, Angel. She's not worth it."

I caress his right cheek with my fingers. "You're right, she's not. I love you, Damon. Only you, you know that, right?"

"I know, because you're my soul mate and I am yours. So now that the chaos is over, what do you say, will you let me take you out on a date, Angel?"

"I would love that."

Why am I suddenly so excited and giddy about this?

"I'll pick you up at 8," he winks at me and gives me a bone-melting, heart-shattering kiss that leaves me longing after him.

But before I start getting ready for our first official date, I pick up my phone off the coffee table and scroll until I find the name I need and I dial it, heart squeezing in my chest.

When no one picks up and I reach his voicemail, I take a deep breath and speak as clearly as I can when my heart is beating like crazy. "Hey *Dad*, I'm ready to meet them. If you'll have me."

When I end the call, I have to bring my hand up to my heart and breathe in and out to try and calm it down.

EPILOGUE 1
Two Years Later

If you would have asked me five years ago, where do I see myself in five years, I could've never pictured where I am now, because I never believed that I could have this. Life with Damon has been an absolute dream. He is dreamy. I love him more and more every single day.

After everything was done and finished with and we settled into a beautiful routine, I reached out to Brody and laid down my thoughts. I wanted to know if he was okay. I needed to know that we were all okay because in the end, that became my end game.

So, I wrote him an old school letter in the form of a text, where I told him everything Damon told me about Eva, apologized for the love of my life being his brother, and asked if he made it.

To my shock and frustration, he replied with a simple, 'I did," and that was it.

But somehow, I understood.

He was hurt, and he needed time.

I know that we will never be friends and that Damon will never be close with his brother and I'm partly to blame for that. But in the end, they were broken way before I came into his life, and their broken relationship it's not my doing.

Every time I remember Damon saying that he'll make me love him so bad that I'll want him to put a baby in me, I smile, because he was right. He did make me love him so bad, that I wanted him to put a baby in me. I wanted a mini-me or mini-him to run around our brand-new house in Houston, Texas, and soon after we started trying, we got pregnant.

Little did we know that our relationship was yet to pass the biggest test, the loss of a child.

Soon after we found the good news, right before Christmas, we received the heartbreaking news that our baby's heart stopped beating and I had to do a medicated miscarriage.

As a person who wanted to wait, or wasn't sure if she wanted children, I never could have imagined the pain you have to go through as a woman. I never imagined that those few weeks that I got to feel that I was a mom, would turn out to make the heartbreak absolutely unbearable.

And that's why for men is so simple. That's why they don't feel the heartbreak we do because someone once said that they start being fathers after the baby is born, while we start being mothers as soon as we get those two lines, and man, were they right.

When I finally found the courage and spoke to Damon about feeling lonely and heartbroken, he told me his true feelings and his words rang in my head and broke my heart every day. He said, 'I promised that I would lay my life in front of you before I hurt you, and then I did the exact opposite, I put you through the worst hell. So, I had to be strong, baby, because if I allowed my emotions and guilt on the surface, they would have overwhelmed me, and I needed to be there for you. You are important, not me. Your feelings are important, not mine. And I know, baby, that it feels lonely, and that it hurts, but I am here with you for every second of it, and if you need to yell, or hit someone, hit me. I can take it. For you, and our baby angel, I can take it.'

And he did. He held me together until some of the pieces fell back in place and I could function again, on the promise that one day, we would get our rainbow baby.

"Hey, what's wrong? Why are you crying?" he quickly takes my face into his palms and inspects every inch of it.

"Nothing, I just got caught up in a memory."

"I hope it was a happy one," he scolds me.

"Damon, we're pregnant," I blurt out, my heart squeezing in my chest from the nerves and emotions, hoping that 6 months after the first loss, things would be different now.

Damon goes through a million feelings too and I can read it all in his eyes. We're both scared to be happy about this, but we're also in it together, whatever it's decided for us. He kisses me, then he drops onto his knees and kisses my stomach.

We can't let the first experience ruin this for us, so we enjoy it and are just as happy as we were last time. "I love you, Angel. Happy birthday," he whispers on my lips and joins our hands together before he leads me to our beach house porch and points toward the ocean.

I frown and have to use my hand to shade my eyes, trying to make out the figure of the person walking in our direction, and when the woman's face becomes clear, my heart melts and only a whisper escapes my lips, "Jess."

I take off faster than our one-year-old Labrador, Blu, and when I reach my friend, I hug her tightly and don't let go for several minutes. "You're here."

"Happy birthday, Nina," she says with a huge grin on her thin face. "I'm your gift," she adds and lifts her chin to indicate my husband.

"You could've at least wrapped yourself, and haven't you heard? I'm Angel now," I joke and tug her along toward the house.

"I thought my presence would be enough even without a bow, Angel," she laughs and when we reach the porch, Damon gives her a short hug and I introduce her to the rest of my family.

My dad, his wife Annie, and my two half-siblings. Jess, my friend, my sister in the skies, and my husband are all here to celebrate my 30th birthday and it is everything I could dream of.

Actually, my life is everything I never dared dream of, and I owe it all to him.

My present, my future.
My forever.

EPILOGUE 2
Two More Years Later

When I walk in the Office building, I know I shouldn't be here, but I had to come. I had to see him just one more time, and not because I have feelings for him, but because I owe it to our history.

Damon hardly agreed to wait for me in the car with our daughter, Layla, but I had to do this on my own. I had to say goodbye when I heard that Brody is now conducting his business from Los Angeles, the place where we met.

"Can I help you, Miss?" a staff member approaches me.

"I'm here to see Brody Mason," I reply with a warm smile.

"I will let him know. What's your name?" she asks with a friendly smile that matches my own.

"Angel Masoni," I say with triumph, even though she has no idea what that means, but to me, it means the world.

When the girl returns and she leads me toward a corner office, my muscles lock at the sight of him. He is my first love after all, and he will always have a special place in my heart.

The girl holds the door open for me and I walk

in with hesitant steps. I had hoped this would be a closure meeting for me, but I never wanted to think of how he'd react to my presence.

He stands up from his desk but doesn't move toward me. He doesn't move at all, like he's rooted on the spot.

"Please, come in," he croaks a few seconds later and I proceed closer to his desk. "I almost didn't believe it when she said your name. You changed it for him," he adds as he sits down.

I swallow a lump in my throat.

"He changed for me," I reply in a whisper.

"As did I," he adds too quickly. "Why are you here?" he adds, avoiding my name.

"I just... I needed closure, Brody. You're his brother, and he... he won't admit it, but he wants you in his life," I exhale and look into his eyes.

I can't believe it's been 4 years since I last saw him. He looks older now, more mature.

"I would never be able to be in his life, when his life is with you," he says after what seems to have been long consideration.

I knew he'd say this. I would've.

"I didn't say you need to be in mine. We don't have to see each other, and I know that it would be a complicated relationship, but you're all he's got. You're all Layla's got."

"Layla. That's a beautiful name."

"It was my mother's name. I... I forgave Carter, and let him go when he killed my sister, Brody. I sure as hell can forgive you too. That life is behind all of us anyway, so it's your choice if you want to hold onto this rage and anger toward two people who just love each other very much."

I rise onto my feet, ready to leave when his next question makes my heart beat a little faster. "Are you happy? Does he make you happy?"

I turn around. Look him dead in the eyes and put on the most genuine smile, because my heart is full when I say what I say next. "So damn happy. He is my soul mate, Brody."

He nods, a shade of sadness in his eyes. "I would love to meet her," he says, and I know he means our daughter, so I leave it at that.

I did what I came here to do.

I opened a door for him, and now it's his choice if he uses it to get in, or he closes it forever.

I give him a warm smile and after a curt nod, I turn around and leave his office.

THE END

AUTHOR'S NOTE

Dear reader, if you have reached this point, you will not believe how grateful I am to you. For giving my baby a chance. For giving a newbie author a chance.

I have been dreaming of publishing a book since I was 15 years old and have rewritten Teen Wolf with a badass female lead character, instead of Scott, and now that I can say that I wrote a book and it's out there, it fills me up with some kind of warm feeling that I hope you all felt while reading this book.

I hope you loved Brody, although he was an ass at times. I hope you also forgave him, just like Nina did and I hope Damon stole your hearts like he did mine.

Before you ask me, no, this wasn't always the ending and she was supposed to forgive Brody, but then while I was writing it, I realized that Brody was selfish on more than one occasion and he didn't deserve her, so I decided to change Damon's role and I am damn glad that I did because he is everything that Brody couldn't be. They both had a horrible past, but when Damon decided to change and do better, Brody couldn't get past it.

On the other hand, if you prefer Brody, I'm sorry. Imagine your own ending to their story :-D

So, again, thank you, and thank you to my sister, also named Nina, who is my number one hype fan and reads everything before it gets to you. She brings back my excitement when I lose it and for that I love her.

PERFECT SCARS

ANNA-KAT TAYLOR

Printed in Poland
by Amazon Fulfillment
Poland Sp. z o.o., Wrocław